DATE DUE

Ferrars, E **X**
The small world of murder
X40288

The Small World
of Murder

Books by E. X. Ferrars

The Small World of Murder

E. X. FERRARS

Published for the Crime Club by
Doubleday & Company, Inc.
Garden City, New York
1973

ISBN: 0-385-06366-0
Library of Congress Catalog Card Number 73–83590
Copyright © 1973 by Elizabeth Ferrars
All Rights Reserved
First Edition Printed in the United States of America

Chapter One

"Jocelyn Foley—well, it's a small world!"

The man's voice was full of surprise. But Nina Hemslow, sitting beside Jocelyn Foley on one of the uncomfortable plastic-covered seats in the departure lounge at Heathrow, had noticed the speaker standing by the bar, nursing a glass of beer and studying Jocelyn, or it might have been Nicola Foley or Nina herself, for some minutes before he had come casually strolling past the three of them.

It was no wonder that Nina had noticed him in the crowd that filled the lounge. Among all the pallid faces there, bleached to a chilled grey-white by winter in a sunless climate, this man's face, copper-coloured and weathered-looking, had caught her attention at once. His eyes were noticeable too. They were a pale, bright blue, a hard, almost stony blue. His hair was straw-coloured. He was not a particularly tall man, but there was a muscular breadth to him that made him look bigger than he was, made him seem to use up more space than he actually occupied.

Jocelyn Foley looked up at him uncertainly. He seemed startled and took a moment to produce a smile.

"Bill. . . ." There was almost the sound of a question in it, as if Jocelyn were not sure of the identity of the stranger. But after that brief hesitation, he stood up quickly and held out a hand. "Bill Lyndon," he said. Then turning to Nicola and Nina, he added, "My wife, Nicola, Bill. And a friend, Nina Hemslow, who's travelling with us. Nicola, you remember my telling you about the Lyndons?"

"Of course." Nicola managed the bleakly brilliant smile that was the best she could do these days and which only high-lighted the melancholy of her pale, plumply pretty face. "But why didn't you let us know you were in England, Mr. Lyndon?"

"Bill," the man said.

"Bill," she echoed with another of those unreal, flashing smiles.

"Well . . ." he said and paused.

"Yes, why didn't you let us know you were over here?" Jocelyn asked.

He looked thin, elongated, and insubstantial beside the other man. His finely modelled, oversensitive face, with the big, dark-lashed grey eyes which could look so alive and so intimately aware of the person to whom he was talking, seemed all at once, by contrast with the vigorous, confident-looking stranger, to show even more signs of nervous tension than usual. . . .

"Well . . ." Bill Lyndon said again. "In the circumstances . . ."

His age, Nina thought, was about thirty. She had also placed his accent as Australian. He looked at her now, and although he was answering Jocelyn, seemed to be speaking to her, with his cool, bright gaze fixed on her face, as if this evaded some difficulty that he felt in speaking to Jocelyn directly.

"I heard of the—of your—tragedy," he said, picking his words cautiously, "and I didn't think you'd want an outsider, so to speak, around. Of course, I'd have liked to see you.

2

But knowing what you'd been through, it didn't seem the time. . . . I can't tell you how sorry I felt when I heard about it."

"How *did* you hear about it, Mr. Lyndon—Bill?" Nicola asked in the thinly cheerful voice that had developed recently along with her falsely happy smile. "There's been nothing about it in the newspapers or on television for weeks now. As a matter of fact, I don't suppose there ever will be again. That's why we're going abroad now. It's supposed to help one forget."

Jocelyn put a hand on her shoulder, squeezing it, fearing, perhaps, that without some strength passing immediately from him to her, she might have one of her breakdowns. Nina found it curious to think of Jocelyn giving strength to anyone. He had always seemed so much in need of what he could wring from others himself. Yet in these last months, she had had to admit, he had not done so badly.

Bill Lyndon snatched a swift, pitying glance at Nicola, then looked back at Nina. Yet she did not feel that he was taking her in. Rather it was as if, being a man unwilling to show his feelings, he found that looking at her was a kind of safeguard against what his knowledge of the Foleys' disaster demanded of him in the way of expression.

"Naturally I heard about it from Adrian," he said. Adrian Foley, Jocelyn's older brother, had had a job in Adelaide for the last five years. "Then I heard more about it from my sister Alison. She read about it, of course, when it happened. She said she wrote to you, then never sent the letter. She was afraid you'd only find it an intrusion."

"Alison?" Jocelyn said. "D'you mean she's over here?"

"Yes, she's an art student. She's been over for about a year."

"Alison—she's the red-haired one, isn't she?" Jocelyn said. "The pretty one."

"Yes—yes, I suppose you could say she was pretty," Bill Lyndon said. But there was an odd look of surprise on his face, as if he had never thought much about his sister's looks one way or the other.

"And she never came near us," Nicola said sadly. "Oh dear, and you were all so good to Jocelyn when he was in Australia a couple of years ago. It was before we were married, of course, but he's told me so much about it. I do wish she'd got in touch with us and come to stay, anyway before—well, before our trouble happened. I understand she wouldn't have wanted to come after that."

Six months ago the Foleys had had their three-months-old baby, Brigid, stolen out of her perambulator in front of the supermarket near their home and they had never seen or heard of her since.

"Where are you going now?" Bill Lyndon asked. "Australia again?"

"Yes, back to Adelaide," Jocelyn answered, "to stay with Adrian and Brenda." It had been through Adrian, who worked in a viticultural institute, that Jocelyn had met the Lyndons, a wealthy family who owned a winery and vineyards. "But we're taking in Mexico and New Zealand on the way, allowing ourselves three weeks for the journey."

"Well, then, perhaps we'll see more of each other in Mexico City," Bill Lyndon said. "I thought I'd like to take a look at it for once. I've been to England several times since I went into the business, but I've always gone the other way, by Singapore or Delhi."

"Then this was a business visit?" Jocelyn said. "How long have you been over?"

"Only a week. And of course I looked in on Alison. I've

4

got to report on her to the family. They worry about all the things that might happen to her in a place like London."

"I hope she's happy here," Jocelyn said. But he said it abstractedly, as if he felt that he had made enough of an effort to talk to this chance acquaintance. Jocelyn had never been much good at talking to people except about his own interests, and if these could not be dragged into the conversation within the first few minutes, he soon showed his weariness of making what he considered were mere social noises. He was, besides, a shy man with the thinnest of skins, who would dodge away from other people suddenly and clumsily, merely to spare himself the possible discomfort of discovering that they were only waiting for the chance to dodge away from him.

But until the loudspeakers told them to board the plane for Bermuda, Nassau, and Mexico City, he could not dodge away from Bill Lyndon, who stood rooted in front of them now almost as if he assumed that he was to travel with them.

Nina remembered how he had gazed at the three of them across the lounge before coming deliberately to stroll past them and put on his act of seeming surprised to see them, and she wondered if by any chance he wanted something from Jocelyn. People often did want something from him now that he had become famous, and his manner, that shyness, that nervous charm of his, often led them to believe that it would be easy to get what they wanted. Whereas there was no one more adroitly evasive, more difficult to pin down than Jocelyn, when he happened not to be interested.

His success was still something which Nina could not get used to. If ever a person had been marked down for failure in life, she thought, surely it had been he. Perversely, that was one of the things about him that had once so much attracted her. Her error made her feel that perhaps she still knew hardly anything about other people. Yet she was twenty-five and at times felt weighted down with the burden of her understanding of the human race. For she studied it, observed it, tried to enter the minds of others and in imagination live their lives for them. She was an actress and believed that this was an important part of her art.

Not that it had got her very far as yet. Sometimes she thought that she was one of the women who have to wait until they are about fifty to emerge into modest fame as a character actress. If, in fact, she ever got anywhere at all. She had begun to have some disturbing doubts about the future. Meanwhile, being out of work had made it possible for her to accept the Foleys' invitation to go round the world with them. At Jocelyn's expense, naturally. She had had no qualms about accepting this arrangement, remembering all the free meals that he had had at her expense in the past, and which she had been far less able to afford than he now could this journey.

The departure lounge was full of noise, of stale tobacco smoke, and of people coming and going, a look of weariness already on their faces, although it was not much past midday. They seemed to have begun to experience the boredom and discomfort of the hours ahead of them, the price that had to be paid by those who wanted to be transported from the chill of a November afternoon in London to an evening in the tropics. Every few minutes the loudspeakers blared out instructions to groups of travellers to assemble at some gate or other. Outside, the clouds were heavy and the light had a dim, discouraging bleakness.

"Yes, I suppose Alison's quite happy," Bill Lyndon was saying with what sounded like a brotherly indifference to the matter. "She goes to this art school place and seems to have friends. I shouldn't be much surprised if she decided to stay

6

on here. She talked as if she thought Australians were a lot of barbarians. Could be she's right." He gave a grin, as if it gave him a certain ironic pleasure to label himself a barbarian. "Or perhaps she'll grow out of it. I couldn't say."

"And what about your other sister?" Jocelyn asked. He seemed to feel that he owed it to Bill Lyndon, for the sake of hospitality received on that earlier visit to Australia, to keep the conversation going. "Ruth, isn't it? She's the elder, isn't she? Is she at home?"

"For the moment. But she's younger than Alison. She's only twenty. And she's—"

But what Ruth Lyndon was, was drowned by the loud-speakers which at last told them where to assemble for their departure.

Nicola and Nina stood up, collected their hand baggage and went side by side, ahead of the men, towards the gate. The two girls were very old friends. They had been at school together, and then, before Nicola's marriage eighteen months ago, had shared a flat in Battersea. At one time the third girl in the flat had been Brenda Weldon, now married to Adrian Foley and living in Adelaide. But Brenda, coming late on the scene, had never been as close to either Nicola or Nina as they were to one another.

Not that there was any resemblance between them, or that they had anything obviously in common. Nicola was tall and inclined to a voluptuous plumpness. She had glossy dark hair which she wore either in a tangle around her shoulders, or piled high on her head in elaborate curls. She had big dark eyes and a rosy flush on her cheeks. Or what had once been a rosy flush. In recent months it had changed to a harsh, nervous red, except when now and then some particularly dreadful thought passed through her mind and the colour drained out of her face completely. Her plumpness also had changed. It had once seemed to go with an easygoing warmth and self-confidence, a casual generosity with herself that had been very attractive. Now she merely looked flabby, as if she were allowing herself to go to seed almost before she had achieved maturity. She looked years older than she was, except for the slightly empty innocence of her expression.

Nina, beside her, looked small, but vital and protective. She had a pointed face with birdlike features, which she occasionally decorated with some fairly freakish make-up. She wore her brown hair short and was bareheaded. Both girls were in trouser suits and winter coats, which they were unlikely to need during the Australian summer, but which they needed now and would need for the end of the journey in about two months' time.

As they climbed into the plane, Bill Lyndon fell back some way behind them, but in the first-class cabin they saw him again, making his way past them to a seat some rows ahead. Nicola chose to sit next to Nina. Jocelyn sat down in the seat in front of them and dug a paperback out of his overnight case. The book was something about the preservation of the environment. This had become one of his hobbyhorses lately, growing fiercer as suburbs and motorways came closer to the charming old farmhouse that he had bought when he first began to get rich, writing the exuberant and romantic adventure stories which sold in great quantities and were filmed, serialized, and translated into the most unlikely languages, and which seemed to be totally unrelated to the rest of his rather withdrawn personality. The nearness of the motorway to his home had considerably raised the value of the property, but he would never forgive that terrible road for having brought the commuting crowd to his doorstep. And a supermarket, too, to serve their needs; the supermarket to which Nicola had been in the habit of walking, pushing the pram with their baby in it, since she preferred this to going by car and said that she did it to keep her weight down. The supermarket in front of which she had one day found the pram empty and the baby gone. . . .

No reliable witness had ever come forward to say that they had seen the kidnapping. A ransom note had been expected and for a while half hoped for. But only utter silence had followed. The police had done what they could. They had seen to it that the press made a big thing of the incident. Photographs of the child had been shown on television. Jocelyn had offered a reward for information leading to her recovery, and endless reports had come in of women who seemed to have acquired children with suspicious suddenness. But these had led to nothing. Everyone had said that a lunatic must have done it, some poor, deprived woman for whom one ought to feel at least a little sorry. And even Jocelyn had once said that to Nicola, as if he thought that it might help to calm her to be assured that it was not a truly wicked woman who had taken their child. But Nicola's eyes had gone almost mad with anger when she heard him, and he had never ventured to say such a thing again. Instead, after a time, he had begun to talk of this trip round the world, suggesting that it would be nice for Nicola if they took Nina along with them, and Nicola, after a little persuading, indifferently, had acquiesced.

The plane was full of music, a melancholy pop song, moaning and forlorn, that went on as a background to admonitions to fasten seat belts and refrain from smoking. The whining singing went on until the plane had lifted off the ground and the roar of the engines wrapped the cabin in a great cocoon of sound. Nina took a detective story out of her handbag and Nicola opened a magazine that she had brought. But after looking thoughtfully at some cosmetic advertisements, she did not read any more but leant her head back with her eyes closed.

After a while she remarked, "Nina, d'you know, I wish we hadn't come?"

Nina had known that she would say something of the sort sooner or later, but she asked, "Why?"

"Oh, I suppose I'm superstitious or something," Nicola said, "but I've an awful feeling something terrible's going to happen."

Nina wondered if anything much more terrible could happen to Nicola than had already happened.

She said, "If you're thinking of the plane crashing—"

"No, nothing like that," Nicola interrupted. "If it did, it would all be over quickly, wouldn't it? I half wish it would—except, of course, for all the other people. I suppose they want to live their lives. No, it's something to do with Brigid. Suppose they found her and I wasn't there when I was needed. . . . That isn't exactly what I'm afraid of, I don't know what I am, but it's something like that."

"The police have the addresses of everywhere we're going to stay," Nina said, "and you can get home, even from Australia, in around twenty-four hours."

"I know, but I still have this feeling that we oughtn't to be going. And if it hadn't been that Jocelyn wanted it so much, I'd never have come."

"Jocelyn only wanted it because he thought it would help you."

Nicola gave a sigh. "Yes, isn't it strange how he and I seem to have changed places? I used to feel that he was the one who needed propping up. Yet he's stood up to this crisis marvellously, while I've gone to pieces. And yet I used to think he was really much fonder of Brigid than I was. I even used to be jealous sometimes because I got the idea into my

10

head he was fonder of Brigid than me. From the day she was born, he doted on her. But he's found the strength somehow to keep going. He's even got a book written during these awful months. Though perhaps that's what's pulled him through them. It must be good to have something to hold on to when life really hits you in the face. All I've got is the house, and shopping in that bloody supermarket, and having coffee or drinks with all the people who are so sorry for me, and listening for the phone to ring, because perhaps one day the police are going to come up with something."

In front of them Jocelyn turned a page of his book in a sudden jerky way and Nina wondered if he could hear what they were saying. In the great humming of the plane Nicola's voice sounded to her only like a rustling murmur, but perhaps it carried more clearly than you would think. And poor Jocelyn must have heard all this so often before.

As the steward came by, he ordered a double whisky, then hunched his shoulders, raised his book closer to his eyes and seemed to be trying to concentrate harder on it.

"I've sometimes wondered, have you ever thought of having another child?" Nina asked.

Nicola shrugged her shoulders. "We've talked about it. I think perhaps we ought to. I think perhaps it's the way things might come straight. But Jocelyn doesn't think we ought to yet. He says wait till we get home and see how we feel then, and so on. Because, of course, he doesn't trust me. You know that, don't you? In his heart he thinks it's all my fault."

"I've realised you think so," Nina answered. "I don't think for a moment you're right."

"Oh, I am," Nicola said. "I am. I know my Jocelyn."

But so do I, Nina thought, and gave a sudden shudder. She thought how extraordinary it was that she should ever have agreed to set off on this journey round the world in the company of Jocelyn Foley. For the time had been when she had thought that she would never be able to bear to see him again, the time when she had been in love with him herself and had thought that he was with her, and then he had abruptly told her that he was going to marry Nicola. And he had seemed to think that Nina would be glad to hear it, as if he had never understood, during the four years he and she had known one another, what she had felt for him. But at some time during these last months she had forgiven him, perhaps because of the way he had tried to care for Nicola, somehow to keep her feet on the hard ground of sanity. And after all, like Jocelyn himself, Nina had had something to hold on to when life had hit her in the face. She had had the luck, just when she had needed it, to get work in repertory in the North, and she had been away for six months, and had had a very lively love affair with a caustic, kindly, middle-aged journalist, who had been obliging his wife by letting her divorce him and who had taught Nina a great deal and returned her home healed. And on the whole she was not a person to bear grudges.

Food was presently brought round to them, plastic-tasting food on plastic trays. Nina and Nicola drank wine with it, but Jocelyn stuck to whisky. He stuck to it pertinaciously, ordering one drink after another. It was not like him to drink so much, but Nina supposed that now that he had got away from the scene of his and Nicola's disaster, he had determined to relax at all costs. He nodded somnolently over his book and showed no sign of wanting to leave the plane when it touched down at Bermuda. Nina saw Bill Lyndon, the Australian, get up and go out, but like Jocelyn, she and Nicola stayed in their seats.

When the passengers who had left the plane started streaming back, Bill Lyndon gave a smile in the direction of the Foleys as he went to his seat, and later, after Nassau, he got up and made his way towards them.

Standing over Jocelyn, he asked, "Where are you staying in Mexico City?"

Jocelyn told him the name of their hotel in the Paseo de la Reforma.

"That's funny, that's where I'm going," Bill Lyndon said. "Perhaps I'll see you there. How long are you staying?"

"A week," Jocelyn said.

"I'm only staying three days. You're going to New Zealand, you said."

Jocelyn nodded.

"I'm flying straight to Sydney." Bill Lyndon hesitated, as if he were trying to think of something more to say to keep him there, talking to them. His light blue eyes, that looked so hard and intent in his brown face, dwelt on Nina's for a moment and he seemed about to speak to her, but then he only smiled briefly and went back to his seat.

Squirming in hers and stretching, Nicola said, "I'm sorry that nice Australian and his sister didn't come to see us at home. They'd have made a change. But I expect they felt people like us are sort of lepers whom it's best to avoid. A lot of people feel like that, you know. Partly they really feel embarrassed about intruding on you when they know you've got trouble, but partly they just want to keep clear of the trouble themselves. They don't want their own nice mood upset by having to be sad and sympathetic on your account. When I think how often I've been like that myself—not meaning to, you know, but just sort of doing it automatically. But it's a pity Bill didn't come to the house. Jocelyn's always said that the best part of his other visit to Australia was the time he spent with the Lyndons. But I don't suppose we'll see them this time. They don't live anywhere near Adelaide."

More food came round and the slow hours passed. Fourteen hours altogether.

It was dark long before they approached Mexico City. When the plane flew over it, it was merely a blaze of coloured lights, as anonymous as any great city seen from the sky at night. Strings of emerald marked the main roads and ruby and gold the smaller roads between them. It might have been anywhere, except perhaps that all those lights had a singular sparkle, showing that the air above them was exceptionally clear.

Nina felt a private tremor of excitement. She usually felt taut and excited when she was on a journey, prepared for some adventure that must surely be waiting just round the corner ahead. But somehow that mood had been absent today. Nicola's deep apathy had invaded her. And now Nina kept her excitement to herself, realising rather regretfully that for the next few weeks it would probably be advisable to conceal most of her feelings.

Chapter Two

As the lights went on telling them to fasten their seat belts, the canned music started up again, but now it had a Mexican throb and was more exhilarating than the wailing that had started them on their way. The plane sank lower and a few minutes later jolted onto the ground of the airport at Mexico City.

Outside the plane, the Mexican evening was warm. It was the sky above them now, instead of the ground below, that was ablaze with the twinkling light of great stars. Collecting their luggage, the Foleys and Nina made their way through Customs and found a taxi. As they did so, they found Bill Lyndon beside them and Jocelyn suggested that since they were all going to the same hotel they might as well share the taxi. The Australian accepted readily and the taxi started the long drive into the town.

By the light of the street lamps it looked just like any other modern city and hardly worth coming all that distance to see. The streets were clogged, as they are everywhere else, with traffic. Tall, characterless buildings, offices, blocks of flats, shaped like matchboxes on end, rose up into the night sky, their flat sides pocked with lighted windows. Only here and there an occasional palm tree or a hanging mass of bougain-villea were reminders that this was not nighttime in London.

Then something caught Nina's eye which filled her suddenly with a sense of a total foreignness around her. A young man, almost a boy still, was running about among the passing cars, apparently at peril of his life. He had a dark, heavy-featured Indian face with stiff black hair above it. He had a long, thickset body, long arms and short legs. He wore a white shirt and dark trousers. And his arms were full of dark red roses. The light from the street lamps was reflected in his shiny black eyes as he tried, with a look almost of violence, of desperation, to sell the roses to people in the passing cars.

They slowed down to avoid running over him, but nobody bought any roses. It made the way that he darted here and there look meaningless, except in some strange, ritualistic way, like a dance with some ancient and secret importance in its mystical antics.

At the hotel the Australian fell back to let the Foleys and Nina go ahead of him to the reception desk. They signed their names in the register, handed over their passports, said good night to Bill Lyndon, then followed the porter to the lift. It was just by chance, an instant before the lift door closed, that Nina looked back.

Bill Lyndon was talking to the desk clerk and seemed to be questioning him. The clerk made a gesture of uncertainty and started to turn the pages of a book. Nina could not have said just what it was that suddenly made her feel sure that the Australian had had no reservation at the hotel and had come to it only because the Foleys had.

She did not think much about this at the time. She was too tired. She fell asleep as soon as she got into bed and slept until the early afternoon of the next day, or so it seemed to her until she remembered that she had not adjusted her watch to local time. She woke to a pleasant sense of warmth in the air and saw through the window a glittering blue sky

16

above the rooftops. Getting up, she had a shower and dressed in a cherry-coloured linen dress which she dug out of the suitcase that she had been too tired to unpack the evening before. She would unpack after breakfast, she thought, as she set off to find the lift to take her downstairs to the dining room.

When she arrived there, a clock on the wall said that it was only a quarter past nine. She sat down, set her watch by the clock, and when a dark-haired, dark-eyed waitress came to her, ordered bacon and eggs and coffee. Jocelyn and Nicola, she knew, would have breakfast in their room. She would join them presently. Meanwhile, she sat back in her chair, ready to enjoy the new feeling of summer warmth in the morning, and found her gaze met by the blue eyes in the brown face of Bill Lyndon.

He was paying the bill for the breakfast that he had just finished. Getting up, he came to her table.

"Well, how are you?" he asked, and not waiting for her answer, pulled out the chair opposite her, saying, "Mind if I join you?" Again he did not wait for her answer, but sat down. "You're alone," he said. "What's happened to your friends?"

She considered him for a moment, meeting the gaze that seemed so direct and open, yet which, it occurred to her, told you next to nothing about him.

"I haven't seen them since we said good night," she said. "They'll probably have breakfast in their room."

"And what are you going to do with yourselves for the rest of the day?"

"I expect we'll go on one of the sightseeing tours," she said.

"That's what I was planning to do," he said. "We might team up—unless Jocelyn and his wife need to be left to themselves for the present. Don't mind telling me if that's so."

"I don't know," she said. "Perhaps we'd better ask them."

"I don't know Jocelyn well," Bill Lyndon went on. "I know Adrian and Brenda well. You probably know we've a winery at Elderwood on the Murray—my family, that is—it's been in the family for a couple of generations. Perhaps you might all visit us there while you're over. Adrian's one of those scientific fellers who with luck might save one from going broke some day. He can tell one about things like mechanical harvesters and the vines we ought to be growing in the kind of soil we've got, instead of what we've always struggled along with. A very intelligent bloke indeed. Brains seem to run in that family."

The waitress brought Nina's breakfast to her. She poured out her coffee.

"Who are 'us'?" she asked. She was wondering if he had a wife and children.

"My parents," he said, "and me and my sister Ruth."

"Who isn't the pretty one."

He smiled. He had splendid teeth, which looked very white in his brown face. "That's funny, you know. I'd have said she *was* the pretty one. She's awfully pretty. But Jocelyn seems not to have noticed it."

"And Alison, the one in London, isn't pretty?"

He picked up a fork from the table and began to fiddle with it. His hands were broad, short-fingered, and looked very strong.

"She's the difficult one," he said. "She's never got on with any of them back home. I don't suppose she'll ever come back."

"Will you mind that much?"

"I? It's her own life. She can do what she likes with it."

"I really meant your parents, the family as a whole."

"Oh, they'll mind all right. They'll feel it's losing her for good."

"Well, sometimes it can't be helped if a family breaks up," Nina said. "Sometimes it's even a good thing."

"It's her own life," he repeated. But a shadow had settled on his face. "You're on your own too, aren't you?"

"I suppose so," she said. "Both my parents are dead and I never had any brothers and sisters."

"That's what I thought, somehow, I don't know why. Have you a job?"

"I'm an out-of-work actress."

"Why out of work?"

"Perhaps because I'm not very talented."

"That's a dismal way of looking at things."

"Anyway, I'm inclined to think I've got into the wrong job."

"What would be the right one?"

"That's something I've still got to make up my mind about."

"And where do you fit in with the Foleys?"

She drank some coffee and started on the bacon and eggs.

"You ask an awful lot of questions," she said.

"Do I? That's said to be an Australian habit. But here you are, going round the world with the Foleys. Why?"

"Why not?"

He gave a quick grin. "It sounds as if I shouldn't have asked."

"You're very interested in them, aren't you?" she said.

"Why not?" he echoed her. "I don't often have the chance of studying a celebrity at close quarters."

"I expect what you really mean," she said, "is that I don't look as if I could be paying my own expenses. I'm not. Jocelyn's paying for everything. And the reason is he thought it

19

might help Nicola if I came along. She and I have known each other for years. We were at school together, and later, when she was a secretary in a firm of publicity agents and I was at RADA, we shared a flat in Battersea. And Brenda, whom you know, answered an advertisement we put in the Sunday *Times* and came to share the flat with us and met Adrian through Tom. Does that roughly answer your questions about the relationships between us?"

He grinned again. "I wasn't asking for your life history. I'm just—perhaps I oughtn't to be—interested."

"But not just because Jocelyn's a celebrity."

"Well," he said slowly, "you know how it is, you hear about these things, you read about them—I mean, things like their baby being snatched—but you never expect them to happen to anyone you know. You don't expect the people you know to be run over by cars. You don't expect the planes they travel in to crash. And you have to have known a few cases of it before you really start believing they're vulnerable to cancer. And they don't get murdered. Yet the newspapers are full of nothing else and the news on television is just a long serial of human disaster, with evil invariably triumphing over good. Yet you don't expect to see the faces of your friends on the screen. . . . There was a good deal on television and so on about the Foley child at the time, I suppose."

"Night after night."

"Then that just stopped?"

"What else could it do?"

"And now they've given up hope? I mean, this journey round the world, that's what it means, doesn't it? They've turned their backs on the thing."

"I think Jocelyn's given up hope," Nina said. "I think in a way that's why he's able to stand up to the situation better than Nicola. He's really given up. And besides, there's a much stronger side to him than I ever realised before. I've known him a good many years too and I always used to think he needed someone strong to keep him going. And I was completely wrong. Jocelyn—oh, he's very strong. And Nicola keeps on deluding herself they'll get Brigid back in the end and so she hasn't even begun to recover."

"You're sure they never will get her back?"

"Look," Nina said, "it happened six months ago. Brigid's nine months old now. D'you realise that if Nicola and the woman who stole Brigid sat opposite to each other in a bus and Brigid was in the woman's arms, Nicola wouldn't even recognise her? Actually I know, because I've seen it, that every time Nicola sees a baby of about the right age, it doesn't matter where, she stares and stares, trying to convince herself it might be Brigid. No, there's nothing for her to do now but what Jocelyn's somehow done, give up hope."

"It's hell, isn't it? Exactly how did it happen? The theft of the kid, I mean."

"Out of her pram in front of a supermarket one Saturday morning. Nicola was inside, shopping. The supermarket's about a quarter of a mile from where they live. Their house used to be a farm once, but most of the land was sold off for building before the war. There are just three or four acres left which have mostly been left wild, heath and bracken and woodland. But there's a lovely garden round the house itself, which is mostly seventeenth century and it's the most peaceful-looking place on earth. You'd never dream there's a motorway only half a mile away and that you can get to London in an hour. But that's how the police think it happened—I mean, that some woman, or just possibly a man, came down from London and got Brigid away into a waiting car and was almost halfway to London before Nicola even finished her shopping. No one seems to have noticed anything. It isn't like a village, you see, where everyone around would have known whose baby Brigid was and started a hue and cry if they'd seen a stranger touch her. The place is a suburb where nobody knows anybody, and there are always a lot of prams standing about at the entrance to the shop with babies of all shapes and sizes in them. Of course, lots of people came forward with stories of having seen someone loitering suspiciously near the pram, and so on, but none of the stories agreed and they didn't lead to anything."

She stopped, wondering what had made her tell him so much, unless it was that he was an unusually attentive listener. Not that there was anything confidential in anything that she had said. It had all been in every newspaper in the country. All the same, something about Bill Lyndon's questioning troubled her. It was out of key with the rest of his personality, so far as she had any perception of it. Whether sympathetic or merely idle, his curiosity seemed too persistent for the sort of man that she took him to be. A direct man, forceful and in most ways simple and not much interested or given to intruding in the affairs of others unless he had some good reason for doing so.

When she had finished her breakfast she returned to her room to unpack her suitcase. While she was doing it Jocelyn came in, wearing a light grey tropical suit. He looked white and tired.

"How are things? Have a good night?" he asked.

"Pretty good, but I can't help feeling it's the middle of the afternoon," Nina answered. "How's Nicola?"

"Still in bed. She's going to stay there for a while. I think she was too tired to sleep much. I thought, if you felt like it, you and I could go out and take a first look at the town, and while we're at it, confirm our bookings for the next leg of the journey. We have to do that sometime."

"All right," Nina said. "I'm ready."

They went down in the lift and out to the street past a group of chattering Japanese businessmen and a fountain that played in the foyer into a basin full of goldfish and water lilies.

Outside, the sunshine dazzled them and the pale blue equatorial sky arched above them. The Paseo de la Reforma, straight and wide, was a roaring mass of traffic. It was partly shaded by tall trees, but still the sparkling morning light beat up hotly from the pavements. But it was the faces of the passing people that Nina found the real reminder that this was on a different continent from the one that she had left the day before. Dark brown faces with strong, heavy features and brooding black eyes, faces that had something of the Indian and something of the Spanish in them and seeming to a stranger, who was not yet used to their mould, all curiously alike. Men and women wore bright colours, except for the aged, who wore black, the uniform of the old in Latin countries.

Nina and Jocelyn made their way slowly along the street until they came to the office of the airline on which they were to continue their journey to Fiji in a week's time. Jocelyn confirmed their bookings and as they strolled back towards the hotel suggested that they should stop for coffee at a pavement café they were passing. As they sat down in the shade of an awning they were immediately besieged by an army of small boys with thin, dark, desperate faces who crouched around Jocelyn's feet, wanting to clean his shoes. His shoes did not need cleaning and his first response to the children was to gesture to them irritably to go away. They retreated momentarily, then advanced again, one or two at a time, their dangerous-looking faces lit up by sweet smiles as they murmured in soft English, "One peso, señor, only one peso."

Jocelyn shook his head and they retreated a little way again, but like young animals, hopeful of a meal, stayed only just out of reach, waiting.

The waiter brought cups of the instant coffee that nowadays is drunk all over the world.

"Well, were we right to come, Nina?" Jocelyn asked after a moment. "Or have I made just another of my bloody mistakes?"

"Another?" Nina asked.

She was thinking, as she looked at him, that either she or Jocelyn must have changed very much, for now she could not think why she had ever loved him as she had. Yet in some ways she liked him better than she ever had before. At the time when she had been most in love with him, she had never thought of him as an unselfish man who would ever be ready to carry someone else's burdens. She had been in love with those vividly imaginative grey eyes of his, with his fine, supple hands, with his oddly hungry, demanding look that had made her yearn to fill him, physically and emotionally, with herself. And also she had loved something uncertain and diffident in him, an extraordinarily youthful quality that he still had, in spite of the maturity that had shown itself so clearly during the last few months.

"I'm always making mistakes, don't you think?" he said. "Mistake number one, marrying Nicola. For her, I mean, not for me. She's never trusted me, do you know that? She seems to think sometimes that I want to hurt her—deliberately, for my own satisfaction. She pleads with me not to. And I can't make out what it is I do that makes her feel like that. Over everything to do with Brigid, I've only tried to do my best for her. But it seems I'm never right. If I'm not callous and indifferent, then I'm spineless and useless. So I'm fairly sure now she should never have married me. She should

24

have looked for someone a bit less twisted up than me, who didn't suffer from my elaborate sort of imagination. Someone who didn't hope she'd think for herself occasionally."

"Jocelyn," Nina said, "what do you actually know about Bill Lyndon?"

The abruptness of the question took him by surprise. He looked slightly put out, as he was liable to if he happened to be interrupted when words, particularly about himself, were pouring out of him. In the momentary pause one of the little shoeblacks darted forward and went on to his knees at Jocelyn's feet.

"One peso?" the child murmured softly.

Jocelyn gave him an abstracted glance, not really seeing him.

"Why?" he asked Nina.

"Only that it strikes me there's something odd about him."

"One peso, one peso!" the child cried, raising his thin voice to a pitch that was almost threatening. There was a passion of entreaty on his face.

Jocelyn yielded and thrust out a foot.

The child whipped open the wooden box he carried, brought out brushes and polish and went to work. He grinned up at Jocelyn, all cheerful charm now.

"You Americano?" he asked.

"English," Jocelyn answered.

"English far away," the child said. "You got English money? I never see no English money."

Jocelyn felt in his pockets and found a two-penny piece and showed it to the child, who looked at both sides of it carefully, then said in his gentlest tone, "I keep?"

"All right," Jocelyn said, adding to Nina, "The expense seems to be mounting."

Meanwhile another child had appeared and had gone to

work, without being asked, on Jocelyn's other shoe. Both children brushed and polished with ferocious energy, giving value for money with dedicated concentration.

"Jocelyn, what *do* you know about Bill Lyndon?" Nina asked.

"Not very much," Jocelyn answered. "Adrian knows him well, because of his family's connection with the wine trade. Adrian and Brenda took me to stay with them for a few days when I was over there on my last visit. They live in a fantastic sort of Victorian house that I suppose was their pride and joy when they built it. A house like that meant that you'd arrived, and they'd had a pretty hard time doing that a couple of generations ago, coming there with nothing and having to clear the land before they could even get started."

"Yes, but Bill Lyndon himself," Nina persisted.

"What about him?"

"Do you—well, do you trust him?"

Jocelyn looked puzzled. "I've never thought about it. I've never had any reason to think about it."

The children both sat back on their heels and the first one thrust out a hand.

"Finish," he said. "Please, one peso."

Jocelyn gave him the little coin.

"One peso for my friend too," the child said with a kind of sternness, as if Jocelyn had tried to cheat him.

"They pick up business methods pretty young here, don't they?" he said, but gave in without argument, handing the second child a peso.

The first one thrust his small brown hand out again. "Two peso, maybe?" he suggested hopefully.

"No, that's all," Jocelyn said. "You've already had double what you bargained for."

Almost certainly they did not understand the words, but

his tone told them that he was milked dry for the moment. They got up and scampered away.

"It's just that he's so peculiarly interested in us," Nina said. "In an odd way. Yesterday at Heathrow I noticed him staring at us before he came over to talk to us, when he acted, if you remember, as if he'd only just seen us. And I know that couldn't have been because he hadn't quite been able to make up his mind whether or not to speak to us at all, things being as they are. But then he asked where we were staying, and when you told him, he said that he was staying there too. But when he was at the desk after us, I happened to look back and I'm sure he was asking if they'd got a room free. Of course, I know I could simply have been wrong about that, and yet I'm sure of it. Even so, I suppose it might be that he didn't know of any hotel and went to ours simply because you told him about it, and he didn't want to seem as if he was trying to attach himself to us. But then this morning he joined me when I was having breakfast, and he sat there and questioned me about you and wanted me to tell him the whole story of how Brigid disappeared. And that could have been just morbid curiosity, only he doesn't strike me as a person who'd go in for that. And when you put the whole lot together, it just feels strange. Don't you think so?"

Jocelyn looked her up and down with amusement.

"Are you as innocent as you sound, Nina, or are you just wanting to hear me say what you know?" he asked. "If all those things really happened, it's for the simplest of reasons. Didn't you notice at Heathrow that he only looked at you all the time he was talking to us? And on the plane too. And if he decided to go to our hotel, it was probably so that it would be easy to pick you up there. Which he did this morning. And if he talked about Brigid it was only because it's a ready-made subject of conversation. Bill's a fairly direct sort

27

of person, as I remember him. If he wants something, he goes after it pretty quickly."

She shook her head. "No, Jocelyn, I'm actually not as innocent as all that. If that was what was on his mind, I'd have had at least an inkling of it."

"But what other conceivable reason could there be for his trailing us around in that half-furtive way?" Jocelyn asked. "If he wants our company, he's only got to join up with us."

"That's what puzzles me," Nina said. "What reason *could* there be?"

"Just the one I mentioned," Jocelyn said. "Nothing else. So stop worrying and enjoy it. He's a quite attractive bloke, isn't he? A little romance is just what you want on a journey."

He waved to the waiter for their bill and they got up and left the café.

When they reached the hotel they found Nicola sitting by the fountain in the foyer, pensively watching the leaping of the slender threads of water and the circling of the goldfish. Bill Lyndon was sitting beside her. As he stood up to greet them, he suggested that they should all go to the bar for a drink, and over their drinks he told them that he had arranged to be picked up by a car in the afternoon and taken for a tour of the city. The car would hold four passengers. Would they care to go with him?

Jocelyn turned to Nicola to see what her response would be. She gave her brilliant smile and nodded, saying that that was just what she would like to do. Yet under her rather heavy make-up, she looked tired out, and her eyes were reddish under their green-tinted lids. This might have been from lack of sleep, but it could have meant that she had had one of her crying fits.

Looking at her doubtfully, Jocelyn said, "Are you really sure you want to go, Nicola? It may be pretty hot and tiring."

"But I don't want to waste our time here," she said. "To go to all this trouble, coming, and then stay in an hotel room, it'd be silly."

"I'll stay with you," he suggested, "and Nina can go with Bill. You and I can go around tomorrow."

"Oh no," Nicola said brightly, "I'd love to go out and look around this afternoon." She turned her smile on Bill again. "Thank you, Bill, we'd love to go with you."

"Right," he said. "Then we meet by the fountain at two o'clock. The driver will come in to get us."

So, punctually at two, they assembled by the fountain.

The driver who came to pick them up was a short man with the short legs and long, heavy body of the Mexican. He wore dark trousers and a white shirt with the sleeves rolled up, showing his brawny, bronzed arms. When he came in from the street he had on a straw hat with a wide, curling brim, tipped forward over his face, but he swept this off to greet them, showing a bald head with the gleam of sweat on it. His features were lit up by a warm smile, as if he truly enjoyed the thought of the afternoon ahead in their company.

That air of enjoyment lasted throughout the afternoon. He was a man who loved his work. From the time that they got into his car and started off, he talked incessantly. He had been, he told them, to a school for guides, where he had learnt, among other things, languages and history. His English was excellent, and his history of Mexico so formidably full of dates and statistics that anyone would have been ready to take it on trust.

He began by showing the party one or two huge and lumpy-looking monuments to the heroes of various revolutions. There had been so many revolutions and so many heroes that it was soon impossible not to lose count. The sculpture on the monuments tended to be of enormous, fierce-looking figures, the women with gigantic breasts, the men with great bulging muscles, who symbolized the different ancient races of Mexico. After the monuments he took them to a glassblowing factory, a small, dark place in a picturesquely decrepit street and of which Nina afterwards remembered most clearly the austerely beautiful Indian face, turned to copper by the glow of the furnace, of the young glassblower, who never glanced up at them as they stood watching the speed and dexterity with which he twirled lumps of molten glass into the shapes of birds and fishes with wings or fins of different colours and of incredible complexity and hideousness.

The car's next destination, after the factory, was the Zocalo, "the heart of Mexico City," as the driver described it, an enormous square with the cathedral along one side of it and the National Palace along another. As the Foleys, Bill and Nina got out of the car the driver warned them to beware of pickpockets in the square. Curious advice, because there was almost no one there but themselves. If a pickpocket had hopefully approached them he could have been seen coming from fifty yards away. But the traffic was another matter. It circled the square in an unbroken, speeding stream, and to cross the street from the square to the entrance of the cathedral promised to be a problem. But the driver, grasping Nina's arm with one hand and Nicola's with the other and looking neither to right nor left, walked straight out into the middle of the traffic, saying confidently, "Do not be afraid, I protect you with my life. If tourists in my charge are injured, I get ten years in prison and I like my freedom. Come, do not be afraid."

He strode on.

Nina felt horribly afraid. She wanted to shut her eyes. She

felt indifferent to the guide's feelings about his freedom, she merely wanted to stay alive.

Then she heard a scream.

Nicola, somehow slipping out of the driver's grasp, had lurched forward right in front of a lorry.

Chapter Three

Brakes squealed. Tyres shrieked on the hot surface of the road. The lorry came to a dead stop about six inches from Nicola. Other cars, to right and left of the lorry and behind it, came to a halt and as heads were thrust out of them a stream of Spanish invective began. Even to people without any knowledge of the language it was all too easy to understand what was being said.

The guide kept his head perfectly. Gripping Nicola again by the arm and tightening his hold on Nina's, as if he feared that she might do something as insane as her friend, he said, "You see, I tell you, you are safe with me. Come!"

While the traffic near them still remained motionless, he strode across the street.

On the pavement he released both girls and started quietly swearing to himself. Jocelyn put an arm round Nicola but she slipped away from him and clung to Nina's arm.

Bill Lyndon looked from one to the other and muttered, "Well, some people are born lucky."

Nicola, who was shivering violently, said, "I'm sorry—I'm so sorry. I don't know what happened. It just seemed . . . I don't know. I'm sorry."

Nina, feeling Nicola's whole body shivering against her, said, "Look, hadn't we better ask the man to drive us back to the hotel?"

32

"No, of course not," Nicola said. "I'm quite all right. Please don't worry. I just panicked. Things went black. . . . It was terribly silly of me. I'm so sorry I gave you all such a fright. But please don't worry about it. Let's go into the church."

Jocelyn was looking almost as shaken as Nicola.

"If you're sure. . . ." he said unhappily.

"I'm quite sure. I'm quite all right. Now let's forget about it."

Letting go of Nina's arm, Nicola led the way into the cathedral.

It was cool inside and the light was soft, but the walls from the ground to the high vaulting of the roof were a blaze of gold which had a hot, molten look, not at all calming to the nerves. In its flamboyance, Nina thought, there was something almost threatening. Its grandeur seemed meant to overpower and to subjugate. There was no tenderness anywhere, no restfulness.

In a chapel at one side, a number of people were kneeling, praying in front of a great black crucifix on the wall above them.

In a whisper their guide explained the scene. The reason that the figure on the cross was black was not because there had ever been black people in Mexico, indeed no, he said, but was simply because it happened to have been carved out of ebony. And the people kneeling in front of it had all come there because they wanted some ailment cured and each would have brought a small silver image of the limb or the organ affected by his illness as a gift to the church. But if someone were too poor to bring a silver image, then he would have brought perhaps a hank of his hair. There was a sadness and simplicity in the scene amidst all the glitter that was moving, and the black figure would have had a stern nobility if it had not been for the incongruous fact that from waist to knee it was clothed in a smart grey satin skirt, embroidered with what looked like diamonds and pearls. Real or imitation, these sparkled with an insane sort of modishness on the image of agony.

The guide gave a faint, patronizing shrug at the scene as he shepherded his party on around the church. Outside, in the strong sunshine, he said, "Now we will go to the National Palace, where I shall show you the murals of Diego de Rivera. They are very fine and are of our ancient people working with their hands in the days of slavery and of the heroes of the revolutions. Come. But please now, do not step into the traffic till I give the signal."

This time they crossed the street in safety.

It was about an hour later that he returned the party to their hotel. Arranging to meet presently in the bar for a drink before dinner, they went to their rooms. The heat of the afternoon, the guide's eloquence, and all those revolutionary heroes, who had appeared in the murals as grey-faced men in frock coats among the bronzed and sturdy peasants round them, had made Nina feel that she would like a shower and then to lie down for a time. But just as she was taking off her shoes there was a knock on the door. She opened it. Nicola stood there.

"Mind if I come in?" she asked.

Nina stood aside for her to enter.

Nicola went to a chair and slumped into it. Her face was pale and moist with heat and fatigue. Her dark hair fell about her shoulders in a tangled mass. She looked with a sort of vacancy at Nina, who sat down on the edge of the bed, returning the look with a good deal of uneasiness.

"Nina, will you tell me something honestly?" Nicola said. "Do you think I'm mad?"

"Mad?" Nina said, taken by surprise.

34

"I mean medically, certifiably insane."

"Of course not."

"But are you being honest? Because, if I were quite mad, I'd be the last person to know it, wouldn't I?"

"Anyway, you aren't." But as she said it, Nina felt a stab of panic. This earnest questioning seemed to her by far the maddest of any of Nicola's recent actions.

"You don't think I have delusions?"

"No more than I have myself?"

"Nina, I'm serious." There was a desperate seriousness in Nicola's tone and deep fear in her eyes.

"Why are you asking?" Nina asked. "What's really worrying you?"

"Well, you know what happened out there. . . . I mean, when I went in front of the lorry."

"Yes."

"He pushed me, Nina."

"Who did?"

"Jocelyn."

"*Jocelyn?*"

Nicola's exhausted face showed bewilderment. "You can't think I meant Bill. Why ever should Bill do it?"

"Why should Jocelyn?"

"Because he hates me," Nicola answered with a sudden, strange calm. Leaning forward with her chin on her hand, she began to talk as if this were a subject to which she had given a good deal of careful thought. "I've told you before, I know he can't forgive me for what happened to Brigid. He can't understand why I didn't take her into the supermarket with me and keep her under my eye all the time. I've told him that all the mothers leave their prams outside and it simply never occurred to me that anything terrible could happen. But he still thinks I was taking a fearful risk with Brigid's safety and that it was because I didn't love her enough. He loved her more than anything else in the world, of course, far more than he's ever loved me. So now he hates me because I lost her for him and he'd like to see me dead."

Nina sat silent, trying to think what answer one should make to something so staggeringly mistaken. All the obvious answers seemed hopelessly inadequate.

After a pause, she said, "How long have you had this idea about Jocelyn, Nicola?"

"Ever since the last time he tried to kill me," Nicola answered.

A shiver of cold ran along Nina's spine in the warm bedroom.

"The *last* time . . . ?"

"Oh yes, but he lost his nerve and didn't go through with it," Nicola said. "I've been taking sleeping pills every night for some weeks now, you know—barbiturates—the doctor said I'd got to have them or I'd break down. I'm supposed to swallow a capsule every night. But you know I've never been able to swallow pills and things. If I want even an aspirin, I always crush it up. So with these capsules I open them up and tip the powder into a glass of milk. It's bitter, but at least I can get it down. And quite often Jocelyn used to do it for me. I'd go to bed and he'd bring the milk to me with the barbiturate stuff in it, and I'd think what a wonderfully kind person he really was, even if he did sort of hate me with a part of his mind. And then one evening he stood there watching as I started to drink the milk, as if he were waiting to take the glass away when I'd finished, and I remember his face. . . . It was dead white and his eyes had a sort of fascinated horror in them. . . . In a way, it was almost how he looked when he heard the news about Brigid vanishing. I didn't think about that at the time, I only realised it afterwards. When I rushed home and told him what had happened, he looked absolutely appalled and yet he looked sort of fascinated. You know, I think that's why he's so successful with those books of his. The awful things he writes about absolutely fascinate him, and as most people are fascinated by horror, they gulp it all down. But that isn't what I was trying to tell you about. What was I saying?"

"About a glass of milk . . ."

Nicola put a hand to her damp forehead, pushing back her heavy, dark hair.

"Oh yes. Well, he stood there, staring at me as I began to drink the milk and all of a sudden he sort of shouted out, 'No, no, you mustn't!' and he snatched the glass away from me and rushed into the bathroom and poured it down the drain. Then he came back and put his arms round me and I could feel him shaking all over and I couldn't understand what on earth was the matter. Then he mumbled something about having made a terrible mistake and that I must forgive him and that I'd better get my pills myself, and he went stumbling out of the room as if he was drunk. Well, I got up and swallowed some of my stuff down in a glass of water and turned out the light. But then I couldn't sleep. Sometimes, even with the pills, I don't sleep. I don't suppose I shall tonight, after the shock I had in the square. Anyway, that night I didn't sleep at all, and about two in the morning I suddenly understood what had happened. He'd tried to poison me. But then he'd lost his nerve and poured the stuff away and told me to get my pills myself because he didn't know what he might do next. And—oh God, Nina, I'm so scared! What *will* he do next? What am I to do? If I pretended I didn't feel anything this afternoon—"

"Nicola, Nicola, wait!" Standing up, Nina took a few quick steps towards Nicola, wanting to hold her and comfort her. But they had never been demonstrative in their friendship. Pausing, Nina sat down again on the bed. "Two in the morning isn't the best time of day for thinking things out," she said. "If I'm awake then, I'm capable of thinking I'm old, miserable, unloved and utterly useless to everyone. I don't think one should ever pay any attention to the thoughts that one has at two in the morning."

"Nina, don't laugh at me!" Nicola's dark eyes were on Nina's face with a devouring, anxious stare. "Please, please take me seriously."

"I'm not laughing! I really meant, *don't* take too much notice of what you think at two in the morning. Anyway, what did you do about it? Did you count how many pills you'd still got left, just to check what happened?"

"It wouldn't have helped. I'd no idea how many I'd had beforehand. Our doctor prescribes a hundred at a time and I don't keep count."

"Did you say anything to Jocelyn about it next day?"

"How could I? What would have been the use? But he talked about it."

"*He* did?"

"Yes, at breakfast. He spoke to me in a very clear, precise sort of way, as if he'd been rehearsing exactly what he wanted to say to me. He said he was very sorry for the incident—that's what he called it, an 'incident'—the night before, but suddenly, as he'd watched me starting to drink the milk, he'd become convinced that he'd blundered and put two pills into it. He said he'd been in a very nervous mood that evening, his book going badly and so on, and he hadn't been able to remember what he'd done. So, just in case, he said, he'd thought I oughtn't to drink the milk. So he'd grabbed it and thrown it down the drain. And even next day he still didn't feel sure what he'd done, given me the proper dose or double."

"And suppose that's true?" Nina said.

Nicola leant back in her chair. "You don't think I don't *want* to think it's true! And it so nearly could be. I took two doses once myself because I'd forgotten I'd taken the first one already. And I was very thickheaded and stupid next day, but I wasn't anywhere near death. Actually you've got to take a lot of the stuff I've got before it's dangerous. But if you'd seen Jocelyn's face when he snatched that glass away from me . . . After all, he could easily have said, 'Wait a minute, don't drink that, I've a horrid feeling I've given you two doses.' There was no need for him to go all hysterical about it. He was altogether too upset about it and he went floundering out of the room as if he was going to fall flat on his face. No, Nina, just for a minute or two—perhaps that's all it was, a minute or two—Jocelyn wanted to kill me and he put I don't know how much stuff in my milk, and then he lost his nerve and couldn't go through with it. But he'd never have done what he did this afternoon if he didn't hate me, would he?"

Nina drew her legs up under her and lay back against the pillows.

"You're sure he pushed you?" she said. "Things didn't go black, as you said."

"No, that was just something to say. He was just behind me, remember? And suddenly I felt this violent shove in my back and I went lunging out in front of that lorry."

"Even though there were so many people looking on, the driver and Bill Lyndon and me?"

"Yes, but you and the driver were in front with me, weren't you? You couldn't see anything. And Bill—I suppose he was just looking the other way and Jocelyn seized his moment."

39

"You know," Nina said thoughtfully, folding her hands behind her head, "I'm not sure if I believe that Jocelyn hates you, but I'm dead certain you hate Jocelyn."

Nicola drew her dark brows together. "I don't, I love him as I always have. More than ever, in some ways, because I feel I've done him such an injury. Losing Brigid. . . . I'd do anything on earth to make that up to him. But still, that doesn't mean he's got the right to kill me, does it? Whatever I've done, I've got a right to go on living."

Feeling completely out of her depth, Nina gave a slow nod and after a moment asked, "Are you meaning to say anything to him about all this?"

"Of course not."

"Why not?"

"Why? Do you think I ought to?"

"It might make your mind easier."

"It might make my mind easier!" Nicola jumped to her feet. "So you don't really believe a word I've said! You just think that spilling all my nonsense to Jocelyn would make my mind easier! My *mind*. . . . You think I'm crazy."

"I honestly don't know what I think," Nina said. "Would it help at all if I talked to him?"

"No, no, no, everything I've said to you is absolutely in confidence."

"Well, do you want to leave him? Do you want the two of us to pack up and go home?"

This time Nicola took longer to answer. She dropped back onto her chair. "No. I've been thinking about that, of course, ever since this afternoon. Just wishing that I could go home and be alone for a little. But Jocelyn would never agree. I'd have to give him a reason."

"If he's done the things you think, he'd know the reason."

"And you don't think he's done them, do you?" Nicola

gave a deep sigh. She put her hands over her eyes and sat there, motionless and silent. When at last she let her hands fall, her glance seemed less distracted.

"Perhaps you're right," she said. "Perhaps he hasn't done anything. Now that I've talked about it, I feel less sure than I did. Perhaps he told me the truth about the pills. And perhaps this afternoon he just stumbled against me accidentally. Perhaps, perhaps . . . I suppose the best thing to do is to try to stop worrying." She got up again and went towards the door. Her body was slack with weariness. "Anyway, thanks for letting me talk. I really love Jocelyn very much, you know, and most of the time I feel quite sure he loves me. It's just that I have these awful fits of panic. D'you remember, I had them even when I was a child. Something to do with having divorced parents, I've been told, and never being quite sure that either wanted me, and really being brought up by a sister. Oh well . . ." She smiled. "When I start getting psychological about myself you can be sure the worst of the attack's over. Shall we meet in the bar for a drink, say in about half an hour?"

Nina nodded. Nicola's elder sister, Jennifer, and her husband had been at Heathrow to see them off. Jennifer, Nina thought, had always had a good deal more affection for Nicola than Nicola had ever returned, and had done her best at seventeen to act as stand-in for the mother who had deserted them. Nina remembered Jennifer from visits that she had paid once or twice during school holidays to Nicola's home, a naturally gay and happy sort of girl who had managed to carry the new responsibilities thrust on her with attractive cheerfulness. Now she was staid and gentle, with two boys of her own, a few years older than Brigid. She had not brought the children to the airport. She had known that Nicola could hardly bear to see them.

41

"All right," Nina said. "In half an hour."

But it was more than half an hour later that Nicola and Jocelyn appeared together in the bar. Nina arrived there punctually, having changed into a brightly patterned dress which looked rather like exotic plumage on her small, bird-like body. She found Bill Lyndon in the bar, alone except for some Japanese businessmen, who were chattering shrilly near him.

He asked Nina what she would have to drink, she asked for whisky, and when it was brought to her, took a hasty, eager gulp.

He smiled and said, "You look as if you needed that."

"I did."

"Reaction after what happened this afternoon?"

"I suppose so," she said. "It was frightening enough at the time, wasn't it? But I'm very tired too. That's the worst of going round the world in this direction. Today seems never-ending."

"Your internal clock will adjust to it in a day or two," he said. "About this afternoon, he pushed her, you know. I wondered if you'd seen it."

"Jocelyn pushed Nicola?" Nina said in a high voice, feeling that to be told this all over again was unbearable.

"Oh, I don't know if he meant to," Bill Lyndon said. "He slipped, stepping off the pavement, and fell against her. I don't know if you noticed, but afterwards he was shaking like a leaf. Perhaps I shouldn't have mentioned it. But I thought, if you're going round the world as nursemaid to those two, you ought to know about it."

"Thanks." She did her best to sound ironic.

"I think you'll find you've got your work cut out."

Nina was thinking so herself, but did not intend to let him see it.

"They're naturally both in a very nervous state," she said. "I knew it wasn't going to be easy."

"You can say that again," he said. "I may be wrong, but my guess is you haven't quite the right temperament for a nursemaid. You aren't indifferent enough. You're in a nervous state yourself this evening. And you look a bit fragile."

"I may look it, but I'm really very tough," she said. "Anyway, I'm the person they wanted with them and I'll do my best for them."

"Oh, that's for sure. I'd say they're very lucky to have you along. I know there are all sorts of different kinds of toughness."

"Actually, I'm the lucky one," she said, "being given a free trip round the world. It's marvellous to have rich friends. About that accident this afternoon . . ."

"Yes?"

"You say you saw Jocelyn slip on the edge of the pavement? He—he just fell?"

"That's how it looked to me."

She smiled with the immensity of her relief. For Nicola's story of having been given a push in the back could be true, need not have been the delusion of a tottering mind, and yet no evil need have been intended by anyone. Accept a little hysteria all round as normal and everything was all right.

"You've been worrying about that, haven't you?" he said. "Well, for your comfort, I did see him slip. But of course, a person can slip on purpose. I can't swear that didn't happen."

"Have you any reason for saying that?" Nina asked.

"Well, not exactly, but still . . ." He broke off as Nicola and Jocelyn appeared in the doorway.

Over their drinks Jocelyn began to talk of plans for the

next day. He seemed to assume that Bill Lyndon would join the three of them again, and during the next few days he went with them on all their expeditions. He turned out to be an easygoing, comfortable companion. He listened courteously when Jocelyn had one of his attacks of talking about himself, or lecturing on the Mexican background, about which he had done a good deal of reading, and even Jocelyn's pronouncements on Australian politics provoked only mild amusement. The two men seemed to have developed some degree of liking for one another. Bill Lyndon was always very gentle with Nicola, as if she were an invalid emerging with difficulty from a serious illness and needing all the help and encouragement that he could give her. Nina forgot why his interest in the Foleys had ever troubled her. In fact, she slipped into believing that Jocelyn had been right in saying that Bill's interest in their party had really been in herself. He generally stayed beside her as much as he could when they were out together. She was sure, in spite of her general uncertainty of herself, that she attracted him.

Then, halfway through the week he told them that he was flying on next day to Sydney.

Nina felt surprised and more than a little wounded that he took no special farewell of her.

But during the last day or two, Nicola and Jocelyn had cheered up and this was so pleasant that Nina did not let any slightly hurt feelings of her own disturb the situation. Perhaps, she thought, Nicola had been convinced that Jocelyn had simply slipped and fallen against her in the Zocalo. At all events, the two of them seemed more relaxed in one another's company than they had been since the journey started and to have begun to take some real pleasure in it.

They kept their days full. They went to Chapultepec Park, in the middle of which they saw the castle where the Emperor Maximillian had lived until the revolution that put an end to him. They bought roses in the Flower Market. They saw young men with severe Indian faces darting about in the heavy, home-going traffic of evening, trying to tempt people in the cars held up at the crossings to buy something from them, something in oblong cardboard boxes. Nicola asked their driver what the young men were trying to sell. Kleenex, he told her. She laughed incredulously. Of all hopeless ventures, she exclaimed, surely trying to sell Kleenex to people in passing cars must be about rock bottom. But it had been good to hear that natural, spontaneous laugh.

Then next day they visited the shrine of the Virgin of Guadalupe, a great church to which people came to pray for help with their ailments, and to which, if they felt that they had received help, they returned with presents of flowers and sweets, going on their knees across the immense courtyard in front of the church. Nina and the Foleys, standing there watching, detached and uninvolved, saw several groups of people making their slow way, kneeling, from the entrance to the courtyard to the church doorway. The pain of their progress was written plainly on their humble, suffering faces. Nina felt slightly sickened at the sight, but Nicola seemed to be moved and kept her gaze fixed with concentration on a young woman with a black lace veil over her head who was edging forward painfully, inch by inch, towards the church door. What awful thing had brought her here to pray in the first place, Nicola seemed to be wondering, and what help had she received? Was there really help to be had if your need was great enough?

They went to the pyramids of Teotihuacan, temples of one of the bloodiest religions that the world has known, but serene now as if none of that violence, that torture and killing had ever happened under the calm, glittering sky. In the distance they saw Popocatepetl with its crown of snow shining in the equatorial sunlight and beside it Ixtaccihuatl, the White Woman, on the peak of which the snow line formed the shape of a voluptuously reclining woman. They went to Tula to see the pyramids there, driving through low hills covered with sparse scrub where the dust lay so thickly on the occasional trees that they looked like delicate pieces of stonework. They went to Taxco, a small eighteenth-century Spanish colonial town, with steep, narrow streets and gaily painted houses, famous for its silverwork, where Jocelyn bought a bracelet each for Nicola and Nina. They saw little girls by the roadside, holding up live iguanas for sale. The driver told them that these were a delicacy, but that the children did not really hope to make a sale. What they wanted was to be paid for allowing themselves to be photographed, and that if they were not paid as much as they wanted they would throw stones at the car.

The day in Taxco was their last day in Mexico. When they drove back to Mexico City in the twilight through the shantytown slums that encircled the whole prosperous-looking town, they decided to go out to dinner to a restaurant to which Bill Lyndon had guided them earlier in the week. For the occasion, Nicola took the trouble to pile her hair high on her head and put on a white sleeveless dress against which her skin, which tanned easily, looked rich and brown after the week of Mexican sunshine. They ate avocado salad, enchiladas, and slices of mango in a rich, rum-flavoured sauce. It was all delicious and they talked and laughed as if there were no memories to cast a shadow over their journeying, and in the middle of the meal Nicola put out a hand and lovingly took hold of one of Jocelyn's.

"Jocelyn, we must come here again," she said.

"Of course, if that's what you want," he answered.

"It's extraordinary, really, but I've been very happy," she said.

"That's all that matters, then."

But as he said it, Nina saw, his hand, in Nicola's grasp, suddenly went inert, slipping onto the table as if he had to escape from her touch.

Nicola did not seem to notice.

The next day they flew on to Fiji.

Chapter Four

They left Mexico on a Monday evening, but did not reach Fiji until late on Wednesday, after fifteen and a half hours of flying. A whole day on the calendar had somehow been irretrievably lost.

Fiji was heat, a hot, moist blanket slapped around them as, stiff and exhausted, they got out of the plane. The night was black.

Fiji was huge, brown, smiling men in scarlet skirts, barefooted, and all with flowers in their hair. They bundled the luggage into an hotel bus, moving with splendid, easy strength. The road along which the bus went jolting was a mass of ruts and potholes, and except where the beam of the headlights pointed, was in pitch darkness.

Fiji was a great croaking of frogs as the Indian porter in the sleeping hotel led them across a lawn to their rooms in some one-storey cabins. In the faint light that fell from his torch, the grass could be seen to be a quivering mass of long-legged frogs, leaping wildly this way and that to get out of the way of trampling feet.

Fiji was air-conditioning that went on with a great roar, gave a clunk and broke down, leaving the heavy heat of the rooms undisturbed, without a breath of air passing through them.

In spite of the heat, Nina soon fell asleep. Next day she had to repeat the readjustment of her internal clock, getting up to have breakfast at what she felt was lunchtime. The hotel had a small swimming pool, and after they had had breakfast, she and the Foleys swam in it, finding it so languorously warm that it was hard to persuade themselves ever to get out. As soon as they did, the scorching heat of the sun drove them straight into the shade. Sitting there under a tree, they drank iced drinks, brought to them by one of the local barefooted giants, who wore a scarlet hibiscus behind his ear. Later they swam again, had lunch, then went back to their rooms for more sleep. And so, for two days, they drowsed their time away, swimming and eating and drinking and sleeping and going for one or two drives in a car with a young driver who tried with tireless sales talk to sell them Japanese cameras.

Jocelyn, who had his very expensive German camera with him, took photographs of mountains and shore, of straw huts and flaming flowering trees. One of these, drenched in fiery red blossoms, was called a Christmas tree and was a reminder that Christmas was only three weeks ahead. A Christmas that would feel very strange, coming as it would at the peak of the Australian summer.

But before they flew on to Australia to spend Christmas with Brenda and Adrian, they were to spend a week in New Zealand, most of it in Wellington, where Jocelyn's publishers had their New Zealand offices. Newspaper and radio interviews had been arranged for him and one or two television appearances. He was also to sign books in a bookshop and there were to be parties. Then for a day or two they were to go to South Island.

After Fiji, Wellington felt as cold and wet as Britain. There was a tearing wind that ruffled the waves in the harbour into white crests. The water was formidably bleak and grey. At first, to hear English spoken everywhere again, except by the inescapable Japanese, felt almost strange, and after having become accustomed to the brown skins of Mexico and Fiji, the calm, fair, Anglo-Saxon faces of the New Zealanders had their own kind of foreignness. At the airport the porter who put their luggage into a taxi politely refused a tip. That felt very foreign too, belonging to a world that was quite new to them.

In the afternoon after their arrival, it began to rain in a suddenly crashing torrent that almost hid the harbour from view and covered the street in a sheet of water. Jocelyn had to go out in the rain because he had an appointment with his publisher, and departed in a taxi, but Nicola and Nina ordered afternoon tea to be sent to the Foleys' room.

As they sat huddled over it, Nina said, "The British really do seem to have got around in their time, don't they? In a way it gives one a queer feeling to have come all this distance and then to eat buttered scones. We really did export a culture, didn't we?"

"Are you enjoying yourself, Nina?" Nicola asked. "Are you glad you came?"

"Good lord, yes!" Nina answered. "This is something I don't suppose I'd ever have done in my life if you hadn't thought of bringing me along. You don't know how grateful I am."

"Jocelyn and I are the ones to be grateful," Nicola said. "You're a sort of buffer between us. When either of us gets too depressed we take it out on you. I hope you aren't finding the going too heavy."

In fact, Nicola was not looking at all depressed at the moment. She was more like her old self than she had been for months. The heavy pouches were gone from under her eyes.

Her plumpness had lost its sagging look and seemed firm and resilient.

"Take what happened in Mexico City," she went on. "That's what I meant about being a buffer. By the time I'd said all those wild things to you, I was ready to listen quite reasonably to Jocelyn's explanation about stumbling as he stepped off the pavement. He didn't think of saying he was sorry or anything at the time, he told me, because he was so scared at what had nearly happened. And anyway, he never dreamt I wouldn't realise how he'd done it. As I should have, of course, if I hadn't been in such an unbalanced state of mind. In the end, actually, I think the thing did me good. It made me realise what mad thoughts I'd been having and that having them wasn't going to bring Brigid back. All I'd have done in the end, if I'd gone on in that way, was destroy myself—and Jocelyn too."

She stood up and walked to the window, standing there staring out at the torrential rain, at the small rivers tearing along the gutters, and the umbrellas bobbing along the pavements.

"I hope he'll enjoy himself here," she said after a moment. "He loves these interviews and television appearances and so on, you know. He always says he doesn't and that they bore him and make him feel a fool, but really he revels in all the publicity he can get. He does his part of it quite well too. He keeps that air of shyness and nervousness that always make people say he hasn't been spoiled by success, but in fact he knows exactly what he means to say and never puts a foot wrong. He's very deep, is my Jocelyn."

She laughed with a sound of remarkable contentment.

Jocelyn returned about an hour later and presently they went out to dinner with friends of Adrian and Brenda's, a couple called Holroyd, who had telephoned them in their hotel almost immediately on their arrival and invited them to their home. The Holroyds were a quiet couple, eagerly hospitable, who had once spent two years in London, where Bob Holroyd had worked for his Ph.D., and who both talked of it nostalgically, as if this had been a magic time in their lives. They lived in a small modern house overlooking the city, and as darkness came down and the rain stopped, the lights all over the steep slopes that surrounded the harbour shone out in a blazing pattern on the night.

Next day Myrna Holroyd picked up Nicola and Nina for a picnic, while Jocelyn was doing the recording of his radio interview and meeting reporters from various papers. There was no rain, but the sky was grey and a wind with the feeling of winter in it came tearing down the valleys, biting at them fiercely as they ate their sandwiches in the lee of the car on the edge of the stony bed of a dried-up river.

The day after was blue and brilliant. Jocelyn had no engagements that morning and suggested that the three of them might go to the Botanic Gardens, which someone had told him was one of the most attractive sights in Wellington. He had picked up the information too that the best way to reach the gardens was by cable car and that the easiest way to reach the terminus of the cable cars was by taxi.

Their taxi dropped them at the mouth of a little alley, flanked by souvenir shops full of alleged Maori carvings. The entrance to the terminus building was a little way along the alley. Jocelyn bought tickets and they climbed into a car that was waiting there. It was painted red and had wooden benches across it at the front and rear, with a half dozen seats or so between these two portions, back to back, facing outwards. It was into these seats that they climbed.

When the car started, clanking slowly up the steep hill and presently passed another car coming down, Nina had an uncomfortable feeling of sitting there totally exposed, with nothing, not even a rail, between her and the ground beneath her. But the outlook over the town, all clean and burnished in today's bright sunshine, was wonderful, and when they got off the car in the gardens at the top of the hill they saw the harbour again, as you seemed able to from almost any point in this town, a wedge of shining blue driven deep into the heart of the city. Even though a wind was still blowing and had a bite in it, the sight made Nicola cry out enthusiastically, "Oh, it's fabulous!"

They wandered through the gardens for half an hour, looking at rhododendrons and roses, at tall, strange-looking tree ferns and scarlet-blossomed bottlebrush bushes, then because Jocelyn had an appointment for lunch with the editress of a magazine, they went back to the cable-car terminus and climbed on board the next car that came.

As before, they sat on the seats in the middle of the car, facing outwards, Jocelyn between Nicola and Nina.

Later Nina tried hard to recall every detail of that journey down the hill, for it seemed to her that by recalling something that she thought she had forgotten she might be able to make up her mind about what had really happened.

But she was not looking towards Jocelyn and Nicola as the cable car from below came up to pass the one that they were in. Nina had turned her head and was looking out across the harbour, and her thoughts had gone far away, as it happened, to Bill Lyndon and to wondering if she would see him again when they got to Australia. Australia, she knew in a rather abstract way, was a very large place indeed, but you were always told that Australians thought nothing of travelling vast distances simply to have lunch with you. She was having a pleasant little daydream about seeing him again, in which she remembered his casual charm and forgot the ambiguous quality that had troubled her about him, when she heard a scream.

It was just like Nicola's scream in the Zocalo.

Swinging round, Nina was still too late to see what had happened. What she saw was Nicola poised in mid-air between the two cars, which were now level with one another. She seemed to hang there, almost stationary, as if she could neither return to the car that she had been on, nor reach the one that had been making its way up the hill, and could only fall to be crushed between them.

Jocelyn's arm had shot out to grasp hers and try to pull her back, but she seemed to twist away from him and fall forward onto the other car. Other people on both cars were screaming and several people on the car going up the hill reached out to haul her on board. She fell amongst them, sprawling. The car went on up the hill, with Nicola being pulled to safety, while the car with Jocelyn and Nina on it went on downhill. Jocelyn was shouting at the brakeman to stop it, but it seemed as if he and Nicola were being remorselessly dragged apart from one another.

Then both cars stopped when they were about thirty yards apart. The two brakemen got out and advanced to meet one another. Jocelyn jumped down from the car that he was on and went running towards Nicola. Nina got down too and followed him. But Nicola stayed where she was on a seat into which someone had thrust her and held on to an upright beside it as if she meant nothing to tear her away from it.

"Nicola, for God's sake, Nicola!" Jocelyn cried. "Are you all right? Are you hurt?"

"Keep away from me!" she screamed. "Don't touch me!"

He stared at her for a moment with horror in his eyes, then

turned abruptly and went striding off up the hill. He was swearing aloud and his white face was taut with anger.

One of the brakemen ran after him. "Hi, mister, what happened?"

"Ask her!" Jocelyn answered and went on walking away.

The man hesitated, wanting, it was obvious, as little fuss as possible. The other brakeman was looking up at Nicola.

"Now just what happened, dear?" he asked in a soothing tone of voice. "You didn't ought to have done a thing like that, you know. It puts years on a man's life. Just what did you think you were doing? Did you feel dizzy or something?"

"Yes, that's right, I felt dizzy," Nicola said with one of her bright, artificial smiles. "I don't know just what happened, except that I did feel dizzy. Then everything went black. . . . Then these kind people were pulling me on board and then here I was, sitting here. Vertigo, that's what it was. An attack of vertigo. I've had them before. They're nothing to worry about. I'm so sorry to have been such a nuisance. Very, very sorry." She turned with another brilliant smile to meet the gaze of all the concerned people who were still clustered about her on the car. "Thank you so much—I'm sure you saved my life—I don't know how to thank you."

"But you're feeling all right now, are you, dear?" the brakeman asked anxiously.

"Yes, yes, absolutely all right," she answered.

"Well, which way d'you want to go now, up or down?"

She gave him a startled look, as if this question had not yet occurred to her, then she turned her head to look after Jocelyn, who was walking fast up the hill towards the gardens from which they had just descended.

"Down, I think," she said.

Chapter Five

The man held up his hands to help her down.

"Just so long as you don't do anything like that again," he said. "Here, you'd better not sit on one of those outside seats. Come in here into this compartment and if you feel one of those attacks of vertigo coming on again, you just shut your eyes and hold on tight to your friend here."

He helped Nina up into the car from which she had leapt a few minutes before, helped Nicola up beside her, then went back to his cabin and the car started downhill again.

Neither Nicola nor Nina spoke on the way down to the terminus. The other people in the compartment watched them curiously and made a few muttered comments amongst themselves. Nina had put an arm through Nicola's and kept it there as they got down from the car and went out to the street and waited for a cruising taxi. On the cable car Nicola had sat rigid and motionless, but as she and Nina stood on the pavement she began to shake. In the taxi that came presently, she threw off Nina's arm, covered her face and started a convulsive sobbing.

"Now you know!" she said in a hoarse whisper through her sobs. "You saw it all. You know he pushed me."

"I didn't see anything," Nina said.

"You must have."

"I wasn't looking."

"Oh God, oh God!" Nicola moaned. "You weren't looking! That's how he does it. He looks for the right moment when nobody's looking, then he pushes me. . . . D'you realise that if I hadn't managed to jump at that other car, I'd be dead by now? Oh, what am I to do? Can't you help me? Can't you do anything?"

"Let's talk about it when we get back to the hotel," Nina said.

She sounded rather cold-bloodedly calm, but in fact, like Nicola, if to a lesser degree, she was suffering from shock. She remembered Bill Lyndon telling her that she was not cut out to be a nursemaid, and if ever she had been convinced of the truth of this, it was now.

"What's the good?" Nicola muttered into the fingers that still covered her face. "I know you aren't going to believe me."

"I probably will," Nina said. "I don't remember that you ever went in for lying."

"But you think I'm mad." Nicola's hands dropped from her face, showing the tears on her cheeks. "Of course that's what I'm most afraid of myself. Sometimes when I was a child I had terrible feelings about other people. I suspected them of awful things and then I used to be afraid I was going mad. And when I felt like that I used to have awful rages and I got punished for them. As if I could help them! But I expect you remember those rages, don't you? I still used to have them at school. Do you remember them, Nina?"

Nina nodded. In one of those explosions of rage, Nicola had lashed out at her in a sewing class with a pair of scissors. Nina still carried a very faint scar from it on her forehead, under her hair.

57

"You'd a rather violent temper," she said, "but you've grown out of it."

"I haven't really, you know," Nicola said. "It's just that I cover it up. And I've got so good at covering it up, even from myself, that I'm almost incapable of getting angry with anyone any more. I'm not angry with Jocelyn now, I'm just frightened. Because he did push me, Nina, I swear he did. He hates me. He wants to kill me."

"What I don't understand is why he should," Nina said. "I simply don't believe he blames you for losing Brigid. But let's wait till we get back to the hotel, then you can tell me all about it."

She was uncomfortable in the presence of their driver, who certainly could hear every word of their low-voiced conversation. He sat there in front of them as imperturbably as if hearing his fares discussing their husbands' attempts to murder them were an everyday occurrence, but he must in fact be listening with astonished interest.

In the hotel they went to Nina's room, and she ordered two whiskies to be sent up.

While they waited for them, Nicola sat down at the dressing table, picked up Nina's comb and dragged it through her hair, pulling it back from her face and peering into her own eyes intently, searching them, asking them some question to which she seemed to find no answer.

When the waiter had come and gone, she said, "He did push me, Nina. I managed to clutch the back of my seat for a moment, then I jumped. But if I hadn't managed to hold on for that instant, I'd have gone down in front of the car coming up the hill and I'd have been killed." She leant forward, meeting her own eyes in the mirror from only a few inches away. "He hates me," she said once more.

"What is it that makes you so sure he does?" Nina asked.

"He wouldn't try to kill me if he didn't, would he?"

"You're sure he's trying to kill you because he hates you, and you're sure he hates you because he's trying to kill you. You know, there's something the matter with that argument."

"Logic, logic!" Nicola cried on a shrill note of grievance, as if she had been offered an affront. "For God's sake, don't try logic on me!"

"Perhaps it wasn't very sensible of me," Nicola muttered. She had put Nicola's drink down on the dressing table and was nursing her own. "But listen, Nicola, suppose Jocelyn does hate you and wants to get rid of you, why should he have to kill you? And choose such blatant ways of doing it too, which could easily fail? You could separate, couldn't you? If he wanted a divorce, I don't suppose you'd refuse to let him have one, would you? Or would you? Have you ever talked about it?"

"No, of course not. It's the general idea we're happily married, isn't it?"

"But suppose he did want a divorce, what would you do?"

"I've never thought about it." Nicola drank some whisky. "I'd agree, I suppose. I mean, it would be horribly undignified not to, wouldn't it? I'd agree if I could keep Brigid. And they generally give the custody to the mother nowadays, don't they? Only . . . only . . ." Her voice began to rise as she realised what she had said. "Only that doesn't come into it, does it? So of course he can have a divorce if he wants one so badly. But he doesn't, he wants me dead to punish me for what I did."

"I simply don't believe it," Nina said. "It would mean he's gone out of his mind and I can't see any other sign of it."

"So it has to be me who's gone out of my mind." Nicola

59

nodded darkly at her reflection in the mirror as if at last she and it were in agreement about something. "You can see the signs of that. They're so obvious, I can even see them myself. But do you know, it isn't very easy to keep your balance when there've been two attempts to murder you inside a fortnight. Even you, Nina dear, might start to jibber a bit if it happened to you."

"*If* it happened . . ." But Nina had not really meant to say that. If she were to argue with Nicola in her present state it was likely only to make her worse.

But just suppose Jocelyn did want her death. . . .

The thought slid snakelike into Nina's mind and although it was only for a moment, it left a slimy trail of doubt behind it. Suppose Nicola's accusations were not fantastic, but simply and perfectly accurate. . . .

But Jocelyn had nothing to gain by her death. Divorce nowadays was easy. Money would not be any problem. He could easily afford to pension off several wives, if he felt so inclined.

So the question was, could Nicola have any sane motive for making the accusations that she had, or was she at last having the mental breakdown that had been threatening ever since Brigid's disappearance?

The breakdown must be the answer, Nina thought, unless Nicola's nature, as she had known it for years, had completely changed. There had never been anything devious about her. But people do change. Particularly if they are rather simple, pliable people, and some new influence begins to assert itself powerfully over them. Could there be someone, some man of whom Nina knew nothing, who perhaps had an eye on Jocelyn's wealth and had persuaded Nicola to help in an unspeakable plot against him?

60

Nicola turned away from the mirror and gazed at Nina with sombre reflectiveness.

"I'll tell you one thing," she said, "I'm not going to South Island tomorrow. If I went, I don't believe I'd ever come back alive. Jocelyn can go by himself if he wants to."

"In that case I'm not going either," Nina said. "I expect he'll be glad to get rid of both of us for a day or two. He's probably got into one of those masculine glooms by now about the awfulness of women. Now let's go down to lunch."

"I don't want any lunch," Nicola said. "I'd be sick if I tried to eat."

"Oh, come along."

"No, if I want anything later, I'll have it sent to my room."

"And if I see Jocelyn downstairs?"

"Tell him I'm not going to South Island. Tell him he can do what he likes. But oh, Nina—" The unconvincing calm of Nicola's voice broke and it started to shake helplessly. "I'm so frightened. D'you know what I'd do if I had any money? I'd go straight home. But he never gives me any money to speak of. I mean, he always gives me all I ask for to spend, but he never gives me much at a time to keep. And I've never wanted it till now. I've been glad he looked after all that side of things, because I'd be sure to make a muddle of it. But he's got our tickets and passports too and he carries them around in his wallet, so I can't go, even if I want to. And if I asked him for them now, he'd never give them to me, because, you see, he's made up his mind to kill me before we get home. It's going to be an accident in some strange place, where people will think I just did something stupid—like looking the wrong way in the traffic, or having an attack of vertigo on a cable car. I'll never know when it's coming, but one day, somewhere, suddenly, he'll succeed and I'll be dead."

Nina stood up. "All right, I'll tell Jocelyn he can go off to South Island on his own and we'll have a few days' quiet on our own here. It'll probably do all of us a lot of good to have a rest off one another. Are you sure you won't come down to lunch?"

Nicola nodded. "I'll have some sandwiches sent up. I don't trust myself to talk to Jocelyn yet. I don't know—perhaps if I've time to think things over, I may decide all I've been saying is nonsense. Perhaps it was all imagination. Perhaps things did go black. . . ."

She stood up and she and Nina left the room together.

Nicola went to her room. Nina took the lift down to the dining room. She found Jocelyn there with a black expression on his face, working his way fiercely through a T-bone steak. His attitude to the piece of meat looked merciless. He might have been furiously mutilating a defenceless enemy. When Nina sat down opposite him he did not speak. A waiter brought her a menu, she ordered grilled schnapper and it had been brought to her before she tried to talk.

"Nicola says she isn't going to South Island tomorrow," she said. "She wants you to go by yourself."

"Thank God!" he muttered.

"She's having sandwiches in her room at present."

"She's welcome to them."

"If you've been looking for her, she's been in my room with me."

"I haven't been looking for her. I wish to God I hadn't got to see the damned woman again. I wish—I wish—Nina, I've had nearly all I can take." He put down his knife and fork as if suddenly admitting that the steak had defeated him and looked across the table at Nina. "What the hell am I to do?" he asked. "Can you think what it feels like to have your wife accusing you of trying to murder her, when in fact

62

you've been doing every damned thing you can think of to help her?"

"I've been trying to calm her down," Nina said. "I think she was beginning to see reason when I left her."

"Listening to reason doesn't come into it," Jocelyn said. "She knows as well as I do that I didn't try to push her off that cable car. She jumped and she knows it. And that's the third phoney attempt she's made to commit suicide, and as I've said, I've had about all I can take."

"The *third?*" Nina said. "There was Mexico City and there was this morning. . . ."

"And there was once in our happy home," he said with a twisted smile of great bitterness. "She didn't tell you about that? The day she tried to finish herself off with carbon monoxide?"

Nina drew a slightly shaky breath. "No."

Jocelyn put his elbows on the table, resting his head on his hands.

"Yes, about a couple of months after Brigid was kidnapped, Nicola shut herself into the garage, started up the car, and lay down on the floor, close to the exhaust. I found her just by chance. If I hadn't she'd have been a goner."

"Did she plan it so that you were sure to find her?"

"Well, no, I suppose not."

"So that wasn't actually a phoney attempt, it was real."

"Perhaps it was."

"Did you think there was anything phoney about it at the time?"

"Oh no, I took it absolutely seriously. It was after it, as a matter of fact, that I first suggested this trip. I thought it might help her if she got away from the old atmosphere where the blasted tragedy happened."

"But if that attempt wasn't phoney, Jocelyn," Nina said,

"perhaps these others haven't been either. In Mexico she could really have meant to throw herself in front of that lorry and just been saved by the guide. And this morning, if you hadn't just delayed her by catching hold of her, and then if the people on the other car hadn't hauled her on board, perhaps she'd have thrown herself down on the track. Perhaps she really does want to put an end to herself."

He thought it over.

"But there's a difference," he said.

"What?"

"At home, when I got her out of the garage and pulled her round, she didn't accuse me of having tried to murder her. Actually she admitted to me she'd tried to kill herself. But in Mexico City and here she's been sure I tried to murder her. Or she pretends she's sure."

"Do you know she's more or less sure you nearly tried to murder her at home with some of her barbiturates?"

He gave a start. "She thinks *that*? But I explained. . . ."

A little late Nina remembered that she had been told the story of the milk in confidence.

"I'm sorry," she said. "She told me not to say anything about it."

"How nice of her." He gave a rasping laugh. "And you believed her, did you?"

"Oh, Jocelyn, you know I didn't."

"I don't feel I know anything any more," he said. "Only that for some reason I can't begin to understand, Nicola wants to have me convicted for murder. Or rather, of attempted murder, because I don't suppose she really intends to turn up a corpse. But if she tries it just once more, God knows, it may be a real murder you'll have on your hands. I'm warning you, because I've had just about as much as I can stand. Remind me sometime, will you, I'd better ask somebody, do they still have hanging in Australia?"

64

That night Nina took longer than usual to fall asleep. Her mind would not let go of some very troublesome thoughts. For the first time, she tried to think clearly about what it meant to be a buffer between Nicola and Jocelyn. It was a role that she had not for a moment realised she would be forced into playing when she had started out on the journey and it was not one that she saw herself enjoying overmuch. In fact, for a little while as she lay there sleepless, she thought how attractive it would be to pack up quietly and leave for home next day.

Unlike Nicola, she had her ticket and passport and a little money, so it would not be impossible to vanish away. And some seedy theatrical lodging in a northern town, the hard work of her calling and the easygoing company all seemed wonderfully appealing. It was a world that she understood far better than this world of expensive hotels where you always had your own bathroom and usually too much to eat, but where your companions were either going quietly mad, or else, for reasons that you had not even begun to comprehend, were hell-bent on destroying one another.

For it had to be one or the other, hadn't it?

If Nicola was telling the truth, Jocelyn had tried three times to murder her.

If Jocelyn was telling the truth, Nicola had tried three times to make him appear guilty of attempted murder.

And neither, in their allegations against the other, had managed to suggest even a hint of a possible rational motive. They seemed hardly to think that important. And every little while they made peace, as they had in Mexico, and seemed to be on as good terms with one another as they had ever been.

So how very nice it would be to pack, slip away to the airport, and get on the next plane to Sydney and so home. . . .

But unfortunately that was the sort of thing that you couldn't do. Jocelyn had paid for your ticket and all your hotel bills, and anyway, they were your friends and really you were a good deal more worried about what was happening to them than about your own comfort.

But what was going to happen next? If only you didn't feel so damned inadequate, so afraid of somehow making things worse by some stupid blunder. If only you had someone to turn to for advice. . . .

The person most likely to give her advice, give it most willingly, in fact to thrust it upon her, was Brenda, whom she would be seeing in a few days' time. Brenda might really be quite a help. In the old days in the Battersea flat, when she had worked as a secretary to a charity that sent help to underdeveloped countries, she had always had lots of commonsense. Not, perhaps, a great deal of imagination. But she had always seen, clear-eyed, the direction in which to go. And if it had not always been quite the right direction, still there had been something reassuring in her sheer confidence in her own judgment, and because in her strictly practical way she was really rather intelligent, it was often· reasonably sound. If Nina told her the whole story of the journey, Brenda would soon make sense of what had happened.

With the comforting feeling that she had already shifted some of her load onto someone else's shoulders, Nina fell asleep.

Jocelyn left for South Island in the morning.

He returned after three days, looking refreshed but thoughtful and subdued. Nina saw him and Nicola meet in the foyer of the hotel. There was caution in the manner of both of them as they kissed, as if they were putting feelers out to discover the mood of the other. But over drinks before dinner the carefulness wore off and it was no longer apparent when they set off next morning for Adelaide.

They had to change planes in Sydney and Melbourne. In both airports the December day was exhaustingly hot and humid. On the way onwards they saw flat, grey-green country spread out beneath them, with a great green river winding across it, turning back on itself, and meandering on again in an endless series of snakelike bends. The Murray River, Nina thought, remembering a little of her geography.

They descended on Adelaide out of the clear, hot sky in the late afternoon. The heat was less than in Sydney and the air felt fresh and dry. Adrian and Brenda were at the airport to meet them. Brenda embraced and kissed all three of them briskly, while Adrian, who was self-conscious about such things, pumped their hands up and down and with his usual slight stammer exclaimed several times how good it was to see them.

Adrian was four years older than Jocelyn and was very like him in appearance, but was even more elongated, taller, narrower, more stooping. There was a spidery ungainliness about him which made Jocelyn's lean body appear by contrast compact and well put together. Adrian had Jocelyn's big grey eyes, but they were covered by thick spectacles and his face had a reserved and earnest look. His skin was tanned not to a deep brown but to a kind of sallowness. He was wearing a red shirt, crumpled cotton trousers, and sandals.

Brenda, also in cotton trousers and sandals, with a patterned shirt, reached only as high as Adrian's shoulder. She was one of those small women who seem to be particularly attracted by tall men. Nina remembered that in the days before Brenda had met Adrian, all her men friends had been tall. But she had never been overshadowed by them. She was a small bomb of human energy, self-assertive and vital. She was not good-looking. Her freckled face, which had acquired a scraped, reddish look in the Australian sun, had small, undistinguished features and brownish-yellow eyes between short sandy lashes. Her short hair was sandy and crinkly. But her sheer confidence in herself usually made her dominate any group in which she found herself. Adrian had always appeared to be happily dominated by her and hardly ever questioned her judgment.

Their car, a Holden, was parked near the exit.

"It isn't far," Adrian said when the luggage had been stowed in the boot and the five of them had settled themselves inside the car. "Not nearly as far as going all the way into town. And if you feel like it, you can have a swim when we get in to wash the journey away. We're only a hundred yards or so from the beach."

"But you're to do exactly as you like," Brenda said with the determination of someone who intended to see to it that her guests did exactly as she herself thought they would like, whether she was right about this or not. "We'll give you keys and you can come and go just as you want to. What was the journey like?"

"It's been wonderful," Nicola exclaimed and it sounded

as if she quite simpleheartedly meant it. "Mexico, Fiji, Wellington—all quite fabulous!"

"I just thought you were looking a bit worn," Brenda said. It would never have occurred to her to have the tact to tell them that they were looking splendid. "Air travel's foul, if you ask me. If I'd been you, I'd have come by sea. After all, you've got the time and the money. It must be nice to have money. I sometimes wish that Adrian would use his brains occasionally in that direction, but I don't suppose he could, even if he tried. It's a gift some people have, and Adrian isn't one of them. Talking of the wealthy, by the way, Bill Lyndon rang up the other evening, said he'd run into you on the journey. It's a small world, isn't it? Well, the lot of us have been invited to Elderwood for Christmas. That's where the Lyndons live. It's on the Murray, on the New South Wales side. We've accepted, but of course if you don't feel like going we can call it off. Only you'd probably find it interesting—the drive and everything, you know. It is, the first time you go, I seem to remember. By now I couldn't get more bored than I do, staring at mile after mile of utter nothingness, because that's all it is. But the Lyndons themselves are all right. Jocelyn went to Elderwood when he was here before, I remember, so he can say whether or not he thinks it's a good idea to go."

Adrian, in his mild, stammering way, said, "Of course it isn't utter nothingness. Far from it. The vegetation is extremely interesting. And personally I find an enormous plain an extremely beautiful thing."

"Oh, Adrian's in love with everything about Australia," Brenda said. "You mustn't say a word against it. Myself, what I wouldn't give for a few lungfuls of dirty old London air."

"Then don't you like it here?" Nicola asked, sounding

quite worried at the thought, because usually it was important to her to feel that other people were pleased with their lot in life. It made everything so much easier and pleasanter all round and did not distract her from brooding on her own troubles when she felt the urge to do so.

"Oh, what *I* like—when has that ever mattered to anyone?" Brenda asked.

Jocelyn laughed and said, "It's always seemed to me you were quite good at looking after your own interests. I've never thought of you as one of the downtrodden."

"Just because I don't spend my whole time complaining," Brenda said. "I've no patience with people who are always complaining. And a lot of good it would do even if I tried it. You and Adrian, Jocelyn, you've both got wills of iron. Oh, it's true," she swept on as Adrian chuckled amiably. "You don't know what it's like trying to make Adrian do something he really doesn't want to. I've given up, that's the truth. Otherwise life would be one long series of rows, and I can't stand rows."

Nina, who could not imagine anyone with whom it would be harder to have rows than Adrian, thought that it was he who had long ago given up. But on the whole, she thought, that suited him, he liked it.

"Well, shall we go to Elderwood for Christmas?" Brenda asked. "You've only to say. Though I confess I'm tempted by being able to forget the whole bloody business of cooking turkey and so on in this weather. Because that's what they do, you know. It can be a hundred in the shade and yet you still eat roast turkey."

"But there'd be no need for *us* to eat roast turkey, would there?" Adrian suggested. "I mean, as you like to point out, we aren't Australians. We aren't bound by their traditions. So we could settle for a cold roast chicken from the deli."

70

"But I thought you wanted to go to Elderwood!" Brenda exclaimed, her voice beginning to rise in protest. It was evident what her own desire was.

"Oh, yes, yes, if that's what you want too," he said hastily.

The car had been travelling along suburban streets with one-storey houses, mostly standing in their own small gardens, on either side. There were jacarandas in bloom along the streets and oleanders and roses in the gardens. The whole scene was steeped in the quiet sunshine of the late afternoon. Adrian and Brenda lived in the suburb of Glenelg, which they said was about seven miles from the centre of Adelaide. To reach their home the car presently crossed a street with tramlines, at the end of which there was a glimpse of the sea, then a minute or two later the Holden stopped in front of a high, painted corrugated-iron fence. Most of the garden fences along the street were of corrugated iron, and so were many of the roofs of the houses, as if they had never quite parted company with the tradition of wooden, tin-roofed shacks in the bush. Yet they were very neat, demure-looking houses, entirely urban. The Foleys' house had an iron roof and a verandah running round it, decorated with some wondrously intricate iron lace.

Brenda pointed at this as Adrian and Jocelyn unloaded the suitcases from the car.

"Either you love that stuff or you hate it," she said. "Adrian loves it. He says it's so utterly Australian, he simply wouldn't buy a house that hadn't got it. Personally I'd like to strip it all off and dump it out to sea. Actually we could make something quite nice of this house if we'd some money to spend on it. But Adrian can't see that money has its uses. You don't know how lucky you are, Nicola, with that gorgeous old house. . . ." She stopped. Even Brenda was unable to go on and call Nicola a lucky woman.

Leading the way into the house, Brenda took them to their rooms. The plan of the house was simple. It had a narrow passage down the middle of it with a glass door at the end that showed a glimpse of the garden. All the rooms opened off the passage to left and right. The rooms were not very large but they had very high ceilings, which made their proportions curious, but seemed to help them to stay comfortably cool. The light in all of them was dim, for venetian blinds had been lowered over all the windows. They were sparsely and rather shabbily furnished, but everything shone with Brenda's energetic polishing and there were bowls of flowers in all the rooms. To people who had spent nearly three weeks in hotels, there was a homelike feeling about the small house that was very restful.

Nina felt too tired to want to swim and so did Nicola, but Jocelyn and Adrian changed into swimming trunks and went down to the beach together. The three girls went into the garden, sat in the shade of a tall gum, drank thin Australian sherry, and began to talk about old times.

"Whoever would have thought," Brenda said, "when we split up in the old Battersea days, that we'd all get together again out here, of all places?"

They all agreed that there was something very remarkable about it.

The garden was a grassy rectangle enclosed by the tall fence of corrugated iron, with oleanders, frangipani, blue agapanthus, and masses of roses blooming inside it. A vine hung in a dense mass of greenery over the wooden verandah, with little bunches of unripe grapes dangling among the leaves. From somewhere in the garden came a scent of jasmine.

Brenda wanted to know what had happened recently to all the friends they had had who used to come to the flat in London. She complained that none of them ever wrote to her, then admitted that she had not done much writing herself.

"One gets out of touch with everything so easily," she said and sighed.

She had lived in Australia now for three years. It had been on a visit home that Adrian had met her. He had been the success of the family in those days, with his good steady job and his responsible attitude to life. Jocelyn had been a hungry-looking young man who had been known to be writing a book in the existence of which no one who knew him had ever quite believed. That was funny to look back on now, Nina sometimes thought. It was really quite difficult to remember those days. But that might be simply because she did not want to. She yawned sleepily in the scented air of the little garden and let Brenda refill her glass with sherry.

Jocelyn and Adrian returned presently from the beach and they had dinner in the small dining room that opened out of the kitchen. They drank a good deal of a very pleasant local claret and sat talking over it for a long time afterwards. Then Brenda and Nina washed up, while the others went out again into the garden.

Brenda washed the dishes at amazing speed, as she did most things, looking as if she was bound to shatter them, although in fact not one of the plates had had a chip knocked off it. She smoked while she did it, the cigarette stuck to her lower lip.

"You know, Nicola's looking much better than I was expecting," she said. "From the way Jocelyn wrote when he said you'd all like to come here, I gathered she'd gone to pieces rather badly, and I was all set to do a job of picking up the bits. But it doesn't look as if it's going to be necessary. Which is a relief. You know me, I mean well, but I don't seem to have a delicate touch. Oh yes, I know that. They're lucky to have you along, Nina. You've always seemed to know how to cope with Nicola's ups and downs."

"It comes of having known her most of my life," Nina said. "But actually appearances this evening are a bit deceptive. She's so glad to see you that she's quite bright and cheerful. But she's been having plenty of ups and downs on the way here. I've been wanting to talk to you about them. I'd like to tell you what's been happening and see what you think about it."

"Happening on the journey?"

"Yes."

"I don't suppose I'll be able to help," Brenda said, "but go ahead."

"Well, it's complicated, but I'll try to explain. It began in Mexico City. . . ."

Nina went on to give as lucid an account as she could of the near-accident in the Zocalo, of the second one in the cable car in Wellington, and of the accusations and counter-accusations that Nicola and Jocelyn had been hurling at one another since. Nina also told Brenda of Nicola's attempt to kill herself in the garage at home and of the barbiturates with which Jocelyn might or might not have tried to poison her.

Brenda listened with a tight frown creasing her forehead. The clatter of the dishes went on until she had finished them. She washed out the sink, squeezed out the sponge that she had been using, put the dishes away in a cupboard, perched on a stool, brought a packet of cigarettes out of her apron, and lit one from the stub of the last.

"For heaven's sake," she said, when Nina stopped, "they've both blown their tops, that's all there is to it. Couldn't be any other possible explanation. Poor old Nina, what a time they must have been giving you. I suppose the fact is Nicola's gone round the bend because of the loss of the kid, and trying to deal with her has driven Jocelyn pretty well round the bend as well. I believe that isn't unusual. I've heard that when a psychiatrist goes to work on one partner in a marriage, he's never sure he's got hold of the right one. It's the really crazy one who won't dream of having treatment. Anyway, it doesn't look as if things are going to be quite as easy as I'd hoped. Oh well, it can't be helped."

"You're sure that *is* what it is?" Nina said. "You don't think that perhaps, just possibly . . ." She could not go on.

"What?" Brenda asked.

"You don't think that just possibly there could be some truth in the things they're saying about one another?"

"Well, honestly! Do you?"

"N-no, I suppose not."

"Of course, you know them much better than I do," Brenda said. "But you said you wanted my opinion, and my opinion is that they both need a thoroughly good rest and plenty of sunshine and swimming and a change of scene. And that's just what they're going to get here. I'm sure it's not too late to put things right. But I wonder if we ought to take them to Elderwood. I'd like to go myself, because the Lyndons can be very useful to Adrian in his job and they always give one a marvellous time. But if Nicola's going to have hallucinations about Jocelyn trying to murder her, I'd sooner not inflict her on them. That wouldn't help Adrian much."

"Bill Lyndon was there when Nicola nearly went under that lorry in Mexico City," Nina said.

"What did he think about it?"

"He said he saw Jocelyn slip as he was stepping off the pavement and fall against Nicola."

"Well, there you are," Brenda said. "It's the obvious explanation."

"But he also said . . ." Nina hesitated. "He also said you can pretend to slip."

"That's odd, coming from Bill. He's not exactly a hysterical type."

"I didn't think so either."

"But you haven't suggested any reason why Jocelyn should want to do Nicola in," Brenda said. "Have you any reason in mind?"

Nina shook her head. "No, if there was another woman, for instance, they could just split up. Actually, I asked Nicola about that, because it was the only sort of reason I could think of, and she said she'd agree to a divorce if Jocelyn wanted one."

"Poor old Nicola, it's all been ghastly," Brenda said, smoke dribbling from her nostrils. "And I used to think that girl had everything. A famous husband, money, a child. Sometimes I had awful attacks of envying her, didn't you?"

"Sometimes."

"I mean, money isn't everything, but it's a very nice thing to have. And that house Jocelyn's shown us photographs of, it's always been my dream to live in a place like that. And having a child—because I don't suppose Adrian and I ever will now, though not for want of trying. Doesn't it all seem mean now?" She stubbed out her cigarette. "Well, rest, sunshine, swimming, that's my recipe for the two of them."

Chapter Seven

And for the next fortnight Brenda made sure that Nicola, Jocelyn, and Nina had plenty of rest, sunshine, and swimming. They lay on the white, sandy beach, growing brown in the hot sun that shone on them out of a clear, brilliant sky. They swam in the clear, shallow sea which sloped out so gently that it was always languorously warm. They lazed in the shade of the garden among the oleanders and the roses. They strolled along the esplanade in the evening, watching the sun go down in flaming colours above a sea that shone with the iridescent glimmer of smoky pearl. They watched the fishermen who emerged at evening to plant their fishing rods in the sand and then stand back to wait with idle patience for the rod to twitch and show that some small fish had come to nibble at the bait. It was surely the dreamiest, most effortless way of fishing possible, if not the most rewarding, for few of the fishermen ever caught any fish.

Adrian had to go off to his work every morning, but Brenda took her guests sightseeing in the city, wandering in the parks that ringed it, lunching by the river. She drove them up into the low hills close to the town, to walk through a nature reserve where they saw kangaroos that let them come almost within patting distance, emus, those wingless, haughty-looking birds that can run at forty miles an hour, koala bears munching handfuls of gum leaves and stolidly ignoring all else in the world, black swans afloat among lesser birds on a pretty little lake, and a very elegantly shaped grey goose that surprisingly grunted like a pig.

They drove out to the Barossa Valley, a wide valley between low, brown hills, that had been developed by Germans a generation or two ago into the major winegrowing district of South Australia. They saw beautifully tended vineyards, dark green against red-brown soil, and tasted wine in two or three of the wineries, bringing back several flagons of very drinkable claret bought at incredibly low cost.

Brenda invited friends in for drinks and the friends invited them all back with prompt hospitality. Brenda and Adrian seemed to have plenty of friends, mostly men connected with Adrian's work and their wives, people of their own age and with interests in common. Why Brenda was dissatisfied with her life Nina could not make out. But, given a chance, Brenda would settle down to a long grumble about her hardships. She could not get any domestic help, she said, and even if perhaps she had been able to find some Greek or Italian woman who could be persuaded to come in one morning a week, the amount that she would expect to be paid made this quite impossible. Then the meat was tough, the vegetables were stringy, there were next to no theatres, concerts, ballet . . .

Nina could not remember that Brenda had ever been much concerned in London with theatres or concerts or ballet. She had been very fond of giving little parties, for which she had cooked with immense concentration, just as she did now. She had read a fair amount of biography and travel books and had been proud of the fact that she did not read novels. She had been capable of spending evening after evening watching television. And she had complained all the time that life was empty and soul-destroying.

The truth was that she had always been a restless person, whose life was a busy hunt for greener pastures elsewhere.

But at least she had the tact not to burden Nicola with her frustrations. When Nicola was there, everything in Brenda's world was enviably pleasant. And both Nicola and Jocelyn responded to her treatment in a most satisfactory way, settling into contented, lazy placidity. It was extraordinary, Nina thought, how often the commonsense answers to the problems of the imagination turned out to be the right ones, although she happened to be a person who instinctively distrusted them. When Brenda had prescribed rest, sunshine, and swimming as the cure for the Foleys' ills, Nina had not really believed in the possible efficacy of such a cure at all. But still it had worked, and Brenda's swift and positive judgment had been shown to be right.

Or so Nina thought until one evening when she and Nicola strolled down to the beach to sit on one of the benches there and watch the sun go down. Next day was Christmas Eve and they were leaving for Elderwood. Sitting above the beach, they watched the great southern stars come out in the darkening sky. The usual fishermen were there with the usual immobile fishing rods, which mysteriously seemed to symbolize to the men some significant activity more diverting than total idleness. The sea was so still that the surf was only a lightly stirring frill at the edge of the blue-black water. Nina felt relaxed and filled with a sense of wonderful well-being.

In the afternoon she had taken the tram into Adelaide to have her hair done. The tram had been full of people bent on last-minute Christmas shopping and the temperature had been in the nineties. There had been a Father Christmas on the tram, dressed in black boots, a tunic, trousers and cap of bright red cotton, all trimmed at the edges with nylon snow. He had had a long, shiny, nylon beard fanning out over his chest, above which his face had looked young and had poured with sweat. At intervals he had called out, "Ho, ho, ho!" and distributed packets of nuts to all the children who had got onto the tram. Most of them had probably never seen snow in their lives. He represented a fascinating mixture of traditions, Nina had thought, just like the accent in which he had occasionally chatted to passengers whom he knew, which was so like cockney, so comfortably reminiscent of home, and yet so subtly different. It was a manner of speech that she had begun to find attractive. It was vigorous and expressive, with a sharp twist of dead-pan irony in it.

She was thinking dreamily of all this when Nicola exclaimed, "Nina, I can't go to Elderwood, I can't, I can't!"

Nina's first instinct was to protect her own sense of contentment.

"Whyever not?" she asked. "I think it sounds very attractive."

"I can't go, I won't!" Nicola said. There was the old, thin note of hysteria in her voice. "It's a feeling I've got. If I go, I'll never come back."

Nina's heart sank. They were no farther on than they had been two weeks ago.

"What's the trouble this time?" she asked.

"Jocelyn, of course. The way he looks at me when we're alone. The way he doesn't speak. D'you know that when we're alone he never speaks to me? He puts on a show when there are other people there. He pretends he's enjoying himself and so do I. But when we're by ourselves, it's awful."

"Do you talk to him?"

"I try to. Then I hear myself clacking on and on in a crazy-sounding monologue and I shut up and we both say nothing.

Then sometimes I can't bear it and I lose my temper and I actually hit him. Last night I lost my head completely and I hit him hard across the face."

"What did he do?"

"Nothing. He just gave me one of those looks I can't stand and turned away."

Nina sat gazing at one of the fishermen who was happily dabbling his bare feet in the fringe of surf. That was real contentment, real peace. Or had he his problems too?

"And you think it'll be worse in Elderwood?" she said.

She had been looking forward with more impatience than she had realised to the visit to Elderwood and all at once it seemed intensely important to her that they should go. She knew that it was reckless to let it become important to her, but she was not going to allow Nicola to upset the plan if she could help it.

Nicola twisted her fingers together, then burst out, "I know I'm not being reasonable, Nina! All the same, this is something I *know*. You do get to know things about a person you live with that you can't explain to anyone else. And the thing I know about Jocelyn is that he's waiting for something. He's waiting for the right moment when no one is looking, just as he did before, to do something—I dare say he won't know what himself till the very last moment—but to give me another push in front of another car or something. Perhaps into that river . . . Do you know the Murray's supposed to be very treacherous for swimming. Adrian was telling me about it. There are queer cold currents which can give you awful cramps if you get caught in one, and there are deep holes in the mud, so that you're suddenly out of your depth when you don't expect to be, and there are lots of dead logs and things under the surface which you can crack your skull against if you dive in."

"Then all you have to do is avoid swimming," Nina said. "And specially, don't dive."

"If I don't, he'll think of something else."

"He could think of something else here, if his mind were really set on it."

"And of course you don't think it is, you still aren't taking me seriously." Nicola gave an abrupt shudder, as if the warm dusk had suddenly grown cold. "If you won't, I know nobody else will. There's no one else I can turn to. I tell you, he's waiting, Nina. It's there in his eyes every time he looks at me. I'm not imagining things."

"Perhaps it's something else he's waiting for," Nina suggested. "For instance, some sign that you trust him a little."

Nicola was silent for a moment, then gave a rather eerie little laugh.

"You're sorry for him, aren't you, for having such a mad wife? Jocelyn's always been good at making people sorry for him. And at the same time he's awfully good at getting what he wants. He'll get what he wants now if I can't think of some way of escaping. . . ." She paused, gazing up into the sky as if an answer to her problem might be found among the stars. "Actually," she murmured in what was almost a whisper, "I've an idea, if I've the courage."

"Courage for what?" Nina asked quickly, all at once overcome by a sharp sense of panic.

Nicola gave her odd little laugh again.

"Don't worry, I'm not thinking of suicide, if that's what you're afraid of. Though actually it does seem attractive sometimes. Just to get away from everybody—away from myself most of all. I'm so tired of myself, Nina. I don't seem to have any reason now for existing. But I don't really want to die. No, I just thought I might slip away somehow and sell the odd bits of jewellery I've brought along with me and vanish. Australia's a big place to vanish in. If I'd a little money to tide me over the first week or two, I could get a job, I expect, and never go home. What have I got to go home for? But it's a stupid idea, I suppose. I'll never do it."

"I hope you don't," Nina said. "But tell me something, Nicola—that time in the garage at home when Jocelyn got you out, wasn't that an attempt to kill yourself? Are you absolutely sure you don't mean to try it again?"

Nicola's eyebrows flickered in her still face.

"What time in the garage?" she asked.

"When you shut yourself in the garage and started the car and lay down by the exhaust."

"When did I do that?"

"*Didn't* you do it?"

"No."

"Nicola—please be honest with me—you did, didn't you?"

"I did not. What makes you think I did?"

"Jocelyn told me."

"Jocelyn!" All the colour in Nicola's face drained away. Her slack features tightened for a moment. One of her hands groped for Nina's and took tight hold of it. "So that's his plan. I understand now. He isn't going to kill me on this journey, he just wants to be sure the idea of my suicide is in your mind all the time. You're here to be a witness to it. Then that's how he'll finish me off when we get home—he'll knock me out somehow and dump me in the garage and start the car. Oh God, why didn't I fall under that cable car and finish the thing then? It would be better than this—this waiting. But d'you know a funny thing? I can't hate him for it. I suppose that's because I feel it's really all my fault. I sympathise with him in a way, because he had this terrific thing about Brigid, much more than most men have about their children. He isn't sane, of course. Perhaps he never was, and all his success and then that fearful loss making it meaningless have been too much for him. Poor Jocelyn. Well, we'll go to Elderwood and we'll have a nice Christmas. I don't really think, after what you've said, that I need be afraid anything's going to happen to me till we get back to England. Then I'll be found one day in the garage, full of carbon monoxide. If I don't get away first. I believe your face goes a nice sort of pink colour when you die that way." Her voice had taken on its light, unconvincing note of cheerfulness and she managed one of her flashing smiles. "But I've probably still got some weeks to live, isn't that a nice thought?"

They left for Elderwood next day soon after breakfast. They were heading for the town of Mildura, where they would cross the Murray River into New South Wales. Elderwood was only a short distance farther, near the river.

The early part of the drive was along the Barossa Valley, with its prosperous-looking small townships and rich cultivation. But later the road took them across a vast plain that stretched in utter flatness from horizon to horizon, where nothing grew but the mallee, a small, straggly eucalypt, which could survive somehow in the waterless soil. Over the plain the arch of the sky was enormous. Nina had never seen such a sky before. No hills, no tall trees, no buildings reached up to reduce its magnitude. It was so unbroken that they might have been at sea. The light foliage of the mallee might have been a grey-green ocean washing away to invisible shores.

It was a hard, battered country, the earth showing rusty red through the shabby trees. Nina found it very beautiful in a desperate way. The road across it stretched dead straight ahead of them, mile on mile without a curve and with almost no traffic on it. Adrian drove along it at a steady eighty. The intensity of the light was extreme, sending up a dazzle from the surface of the road. The air was hot and parched and dusty.

Before they reached Mildura they returned to a kindlier country of vineyards and orchards of citrus and apricots. They had a picnic lunch on the way and it was midafternoon when they entered Mildura and crossed the river. The remainder of the drive took less than an hour. Elderwood itself consisted of little but a single street of one-storey houses, most of them roofed with corrugated iron, some of them shops with canopies built out from them to shade the pavements, some of them pubs, one of them a garage. A two-storey building of wood, decorated with a great deal of iron lace, was the town's one hotel. The street was wide and almost empty, except for a few dogs nosing about in the dust.

It was the Lyndons' dogs that first came to meet them when they turned into the drive that led up to the house, a drive between two rows of graceful Norfolk Island pines. Nina had always believed that the British were the people most addicted to dog-loving in the world, but had never in her life seen as many dogs per person as she had in Australia. The Lyndons' dogs were a Labrador and a toy poodle and they came racing towards the car in an ecstasy of interest in these strangers who had come visiting. Both barked a frenzied greeting in which the shrill yelping of the little poodle almost drowned the deeper uproar of the bigger dog.

The house was on a slight eminence, a knoll that was the nearest thing to a hill in all the country round. It was a very solid-looking house of two storeys, built of brick, and was really a very ugly one, ornate yet graceless, but it had certain dignity. In a way it was imposing. Standing there on its hillock with its fine avenue of pines and a beautifully kept garden laid out around it, it dominated the immediate landscape with a look of sober opulence, of high quality, of having had nothing but the best used in its construction. Except that it had a roof of corrugated iron. In these parts that seemed unavoidable.

The noise that the dogs were making brought Bill Lyndon out of the house. As Jocelyn got out of the car, the big Labrador, thumping his tail, put his paws up on his chest and reached for his face with a long pink tongue.

"It almost looks as if he recognises you, Jocelyn," Bill said, "though it doesn't seem possible, after nearly two years. He was Alison's, d'you remember? He fretted for weeks after she went to Europe, then he attached himself to me. The poodle's officially Ruth's, but he's so jealous, he follows us around. And I'm not really an animal lover. How was the drive? Pretty hot?"

Bill picked up two of the suitcases and started up the steps to the door.

As he did so, a tall middle-aged woman came hurrying out of the door and plunged down the steps.

"Brenda!" she exclaimed and engulfed her in a strenuous embrace, with kisses. "Lovely to see you, lovey! And Adrian. And Jocelyn—I always knew you'd be back sooner or later." She kissed both of them too. "And Nicola—this is Nicola?"

Her son told her no, that that was Nina.

Nina was warmly kissed and welcomed.

Then Bill's mother turned to Nicola who was standing by the car and for a moment the older woman hesitated. Then she put an arm round Nicola's shoulders and drew her up the steps ahead of the others.

"That long hot drive—you must be very tired," she said. "Come in and we'll have some tea."

Winnie Lyndon was broad and muscular-looking as well as tall, with a jerky impulsiveness in her movements. She had light blue eyes, like her son's, in a leathery, square face with

86

a wide, pleasant mouth, on which there was a good deal of carelessly applied orange lipstick. Her thick grey hair was piled up somehow on her head, with strands of it straggling down her neck. Her skin was shiny from the heat. She wore a cotton dress, very short for her age, with a bright flowery pattern on it. Her bare legs were long and strong and brown.

"We'll have tea on the verandah at the back," she said. "It's shady there and nice and cool."

"Thank you, that sounds very nice," Nicola answered. She had been in a curious mood all day, quiet and vague. It was as if, having come to the conclusion that she was not in any danger until she got home, she had stopped caring about anything.

"We're so glad you could come," Winnie Lyndon went on. "I like to have visitors for Christmas. It must seem very strange to you, Christmas in this heat. I remember a Christmas in London once when I was a girl. It was a wartime Christmas. I was a nurse. There were air raids, but they'd somehow got hold of some turkeys at the hospital where I was working and we dished out quite a good Christmas dinner for the patients. I haven't been back to Europe since. I don't know why, but since I married I always seem to have had too much to do to go travelling. I've a daughter in London now, you know. She's an art student."

Chatting, she led Nicola into the hall and up the wide staircase. It had a heavy balustrade fantastically carved with fruit and flowers, at the bottom of which, on the newel post, a modestly draped nymph held aloft a light with a glass shade shaped like a flaming torch. The others followed and were taken to their rooms.

Nina's was as wondrously a period piece as the rest of the house. There was a brass bedstead, a great rosewood wardrobe, a dressing table to match, a carpet with a pattern of cabbage roses, paintings on the walls of mountains, stags, and Highland cattle, and there were medallions of stained glass in the windows depicting lochs and castles. Alone in the room, she felt what a bewildering incongruity there was about having come such a distance only to find that she had simply taken a step backwards into Victorian England.

She unpacked her one case, took off the cotton dress, crumpled by the long, hot drive, in which she had arrived, put on a silk dress in cool green and white stripes, spent a good deal of time on her hair and her make-up, then went downstairs. As she had hoped but not really expected, she found Bill on the verandah alone. He was standing with his back to her, leaning against one of the uprights that supported the roof of the verandah, and was gazing across the garden, a long strip of lawn that sloped down to a belt of trees, with tall shrubs and roses to left and right of it. Hearing Nina's footsteps, he turned. His eyes, of the same colour as his mother's but with the stony quality that Nina remembered and that his mother's lacked, lit up for a moment when he saw her, and she was expecting him to say something about its being good to see her again when he said abruptly, "Nina, that friend of yours, Nicola—what's the matter with her now? She's looking worse than she did in Mexico. Has that struck you, or are you too close to see it?"

Nina sat down on one of the basket chairs on the verandah. She said with exasperation, "Bill, d'you know that whenever I see you, you do nothing but ask me questions about the Foleys? Actually I was thinking I wanted to talk to you about them, but your obsession with them makes me feel perhaps I don't. It's something I don't understand. It makes me uncomfortable."

"I'm sorry," he said. "I didn't realise it seemed like an obsession."

88

"Well, it does. And there's another thing. When you first spoke to us at Heathrow, looking so surprised to see Jocelyn, you'd really been looking at him for some minutes before you decided to come over. That surprise was quite put on. So what's it all about?"

He smiled. "All right, the surprise was put on. But there's a simple enough explanation of it."

"That one about being afraid of intruding? You weren't in the least afraid. You stuck close enough to us in Mexico City."

"But that's covered by the same explanation. What happened at Heathrow is that I saw the three of you across the departure lounge and recognised Jocelyn, and I deduced that one of the women with him was his wife and the other a friend. And if the unattached one was you I wanted to get acquainted, but if you were Jocelyn's wife, then I was going to be very delicate and not intrude, because Nicola's a very sweet and charming girl, but at the best of times she's not the kind that does anything to me. Now are you satisfied?"

"No."

"You take a lot of convincing."

Nina smiled up at him as he stood with his wide shoulders propped against the upright of the verandah.

"I think it's Jocelyn you're interested in, not me."

"It was you I stuck close to when I could in Mexico."

"Because of the Foleys."

"No. Well, at first, perhaps. Not afterwards."

"But you've a very curious interest in them. When I came out here just now, the first thing you asked me was what was wrong with Nicola. Bill, please . . ." Her voice changed suddenly to a tone of anxious seriousness. "You've got something on your mind about them and I've got an awful lot on mine. Can't you help me? There was a thing that happened in New Zealand. . . . Nicola nearly fell off a cable car in front of another, and afterwards she said Jocelyn pushed her, just as she did in Mexico. But if he did, he's insane, because he's got no possible reason for wanting to kill her. And if he didn't, then Nicola's insane, because she's making up these awful things about him without any rational motive. And I feel so responsible for them both. So won't you tell me why you of all people should be worried about them? I mean, you don't know either of them very well; you come from the other side of the world, and you haven't had anything to do with either of them for ages."

His smile had faded as he listened to her and a distant look had settled on his face. It was almost a look of hostility, as if he resented her appeal.

After a slight pause, he said, "I'd like to tell you everything I've got on my mind, but it isn't good to talk of some things when you aren't sure of them. It can do an awful lot of damage. Particularly if there's a question of loyalty involved. Let's leave it at that. I'm sorry."

"Loyalty to whom?"

"Never mind. I shouldn't have said that."

"Oh, now you've only made things worse!" she exclaimed. "It's as if you know something discreditable or even dangerous about Jocelyn or Nicola, or you feel something, or guess something—"

He stopped her with a hand on her shoulder.

"I told you, I can't talk about it, Nina. I'm very sorry. I'll say just one thing. I think it might help you if you stopped thinking of either of them as insane. Try taking the sanity of both of them for granted. That's what I'm doing. I'm assuming there are good reasons for the way they've acted."

"What good reasons?"

He did not answer.

"You make it sound terrifying," she said in a low voice.

"Perhaps it is. Yes, I should say it might be terrifying."

His hand dropped from her shoulder and he turned away as voices sounded from among the trees at the bottom of the garden.

Chapter Eight

A small elderly man and a tall young girl emerged from the trees. They were followed by a young man, a gangling figure with reddish hair that curled down over his collar and green eyes in an open, blunt-featured face.

The girl was about twenty. She was slender and delicately built, yet gawky with it, as if she had not wholly outgrown her adolescence. She had long pale golden hair, negligently caught back from her face by a ribbon. The pretty one of the family, Nina remembered her brother calling her, and Ruth Lyndon was certainly very pretty. But there was a petulance about her small, pointed face that detracted from its charm. She looked as if she had some grievance on her mind which she enjoyed cherishing.

The older man, Henry Lyndon, was about sixty and was rather like a shrunken edition of his son, Bill, very spare and light and several inches the shorter. But he had a strong, determined face. He had a high, ridged forehead and a freckled top to his head, sparsely fringed with silvery hair.

Bill introduced the three of them to Nina. The young man's name was Ern Wilding and his family were graziers who owned a sheep station not far away. When presently Brenda, Adrian, Jocelyn, Nicola, Winnie Lyndon, and the two dogs had joined the group, tea was brought out by a slim, middle-aged woman with a strong Lancashire accent. She wore a white nylon overall and was introduced as Mrs. Bollard, the housekeeper, a widow who had come to Australia to be near her son and his family, who lived in Mildura. Refusing tea, Ern Wilding said that they must all come over to see his parents, say on Boxing Day, bent over Winnie Lyndon, kissed her on the cheek and walked off to his car. Ruth went with him and they disappeared round the corner of the house together.

"They're engaged," Winnie Lyndon explained to the visitors. "More or less, at any rate. They're taking their time, making up their minds. I used to think Ern would marry Alison before she went away, but once she went, he switched to Ruth straight off. So I think perhaps it was really Ruth all along."

"Now for God's sake, don't let her hear you say any of that," her husband said. "If she gets it into her head she's second best to Alison, she'll never make up her mind. She'll decide she's got to go to Europe too, just to show she's got it in her, and we'll lose them both. And Ern's a nice boy and it would be nice for us all to have her settled only twenty miles away."

"Well, she won't leave for the same reason as Alison, that's for sure," Winnie Lyndon said as she poured out tea. "Not Ruth. She's got her head screwed on all right. She'll look before she leaps."

"Mother!" her husband said with a note of warning in his voice.

She gave him back a long, steady look.

"Now listen," she said, "we're among friends, and I can tell you there's something I won't do, and that's keep off talking about my own daughter even when we're among friends. I know it's been a shock, what Bill found out when he went over there, but let me tell you, almost the worst part of the shock to me was that the poor child felt she couldn't tell us anything about it. And now we've got to accept it and live with it. So don't 'Mother!' me like that, as if we were a lot of fools who can't look facts in the face." Her glance swept round the circle of people on the verandah. "We've found out, you see, why Alison really went away. She was pregnant and she didn't want us to know. And how long it would have been before we found out, if Bill hadn't happened to go to see her, I don't know. The child's six months old already. Can you imagine that? I mean, Alison going through all that alone and being afraid to tell us. It breaks my heart to think of it. Of course, I ought to have realised it before she went. I blame myself. She was three months gone already. But she's one of those strongly built people who never show it much. I never showed it much till the last month or so when I had the children. And she refuses to say who the father was and says anyway she'd never think of marrying him and she's going to bring up the child all alone and won't even think of having it adopted—because that's what Bill suggested she should do, but she wouldn't listen to him, any more than I should have myself. Well, there you are, that's the story and I'm sad and sorry about it, but I'm not going to make it a dark secret. And I'll tell you one thing, if Alison won't come home, then one day I'm going to pack up and go over to London myself, because I want to see my grandchild. . . ." She broke off as Ruth reappeared round the corner of the house. "Don't talk about it in front of Ruth," she muttered. "It upsets her."

But although she had dropped her voice, Ruth had heard her as she came with her gawky, adolescent strides towards the verandah.

"You're talking about Alison again," she said in a surly

94

tone. "Go on, if you must. Personally, I'm sick and tired of the subject. We've talked about nothing else since Bill got home. And all that whispering about who the father was, which I'm not supposed to hear—all right, suppose it was Ern, what difference does that make to me? You don't suppose I think I'm the first woman in his life. I shouldn't like to be, as a matter of fact. If I were, I'd be wondering if he was really a queer. But I don't think he *is* the father of the child, because he's told me he isn't and I happen to believe him. And you can call me naïve, if you want to, believing the word of the man I'm in love with, but that happens to be how I am. And Alison and her baby can go to hell for all I care!"

There was a childish forlornness in her final exclamation as she swung round and strode into the house.

"Oh dear," Winnie Lyndon said, "of course she does believe Ern's the father and it's tearing her to pieces. She's trying to be loyal to him, but she doesn't know if she can forgive him or not. Those other women in his life, if they ever existed, don't mean anything to her because she never saw them, she can't really imagine them. Oh, my two poor girls, what a mess they do seem to be making of their lives! Nicola, lovey, some more tea."

Dreamily, Nicola handed over her cup. If she had taken in what she had heard, she gave no sign of it. She might have been sitting alone on the verandah, listening to the birds singing in the garden. Jocelyn was looking embarrassed at the display of so much uninhibited emotion, Adrian was looking distressed, Brenda seemed deeply interested. Ruth's father was shaking his head gravely at so much having been said that he considered unnecessary. Nina noticed that he had a strong, firmly moulded mouth and that the way his lips closed gave him the appearance of being able to keep in everything that it was not essential to say. She noticed too that Bill was watching her steadily, searching her face for something.

Suddenly a new thought shot into her mind and exploded there with a violence that made the hand holding her teacup shake faintly and slop some tea into the saucer. Could Bill believe that Jocelyn was the father of Alison's child? Did that explain Bill's curious interest in him? Jocelyn had been a guest of the Lyndons' once before. He had known Alison. Was that why Bill believed that Jocelyn could have a sane reason for trying to get rid of Nicola? Did he think that Jocelyn wanted to marry Alison and have the paternity of his second child recognised in place of the one that he had lost?

But that was nonsense. Apart from the fact that Nicola had said that she would divorce him if he wanted it, there was the fact that it was nearly two years since Jocelyn's former visit to Australia and Alison had not become pregnant until three months before she left for London, about a year later. The thing was physically impossible. If that was the suspicion that was worrying Bill, it would be simple to re-assure him.

Only he was certainly as capable of doing arithmetic as Nina was.

So was he watching her in that absorbed way for some quite different reason, for instance, just because it gave him pleasure? Why couldn't she think about that for a little, instead of brooding on other people's problems?

Dinner that evening was fairly late and proceeded slowly, with long pauses between the courses. The dining room was a sombre room with dark panelling, dark velvet curtains, a remarkably carved black marble mantelpiece, a vast dining table, a sideboard that could have housed a family, and heavy mahogany chairs. A gilt clock under a glass bell ticked on the mantelpiece.

They ate a delicious kind of fresh-water crayfish, huge T-bone steaks that looked magnificent but were actually fearsomely tough, and luscious strawberries and cream. The talk soon became technical and was mostly between the men. They talked of the rising cost of labour in the vineyards, of the revolution caused by mechanical harvesting, of irrigation, of desalination, of the wines of the Barossa, of the Hunter Valley, of Mildura. They drank one of the Lyndons' own wines, a Shiraz, and later brandy. It was half past eleven by the time they left the table.

Nina went up to bed as soon afterwards as she could, but almost as soon as she closed the door behind her, there was a tap on it and Nicola came in. Without saying anything, she strolled across the room to the window, which was open, and peered out into the dark garden through the wire screen.

Nina waited for her to say why she had come.

After a little Nicola said, "It's nice here, isn't it? I like these people."

Nina unzipped her dress and let it slide off her shoulders to the floor.

"Then you're glad you came?"

"Oh yes, aren't you?"

"Oh, *I'm* glad," Nina said. "But I thought you were frightened of coming."

"Not any more. Not since you told me that story Jocelyn made up about me trying to kill myself in the garage. I think his telling you that means he's given up the idea of killing me on this journey. And I think I can look after myself once we're home. But anyway, one couldn't feel frightened here. They're all so good. Especially Mrs. Lyndon. The way she talked about Alison. I like that. I think the girl must be a fool not to come home."

"There might be problems between her and Ruth about Ern Wilding."

"I suppose so. Of course, I understand now why she didn't come to see us. She must have thought we mightn't want to see her if she'd an illegitimate child. An irony, isn't it?"

"Sad, but why specially an irony?" Nina asked.

"Why, because of Jocelyn and me and the way things happened."

"The way what things happened?"

"Do you mean you don't know?"

"I don't know what you're talking about."

"But I always thought you knew. I thought he told you. He said he had. Well, never mind. It's late, I'll leave you in peace. Good night." Nicola seemed suddenly in a hurry to leave.

"Just a minute," Nina said. "What were you trying to say to me?"

"Nothing," Nicola said. "Nothing that matters."

"What was it?"

Nicola shrugged her shoulders. "I was only talking about how Jocelyn and I got married. And we never should have, that's so clear now. He ought to have married you. It was you he was in love with. And if I'd had the courage of that girl Alison, we shouldn't be in the mess we're in now. You really mean you didn't know . . . ?" Seeing Nina's blank face, Nicola's voice faltered. "Well, if you want me to spell it out, a bit after Jocelyn got back from Australia we were alone in the flat and I got him to make love to me. I was terribly in love with him, didn't you know that? So I didn't care what I did. All the same, I don't think things would have gone any farther if I hadn't started to have Brigid and told Jocelyn about it, and straightaway he said we'd get married and he seemed quite happy about it. He did want a child, you see, that was awfully important to him, even if he didn't much want me. But I made myself think he loved me and I believe he made himself think so too until recently. . . ." She yawned exhaustedly. "I must remember to get Alison's address from Mrs. Lyndon so that we can write to her when we get home. Oh God, I'm so tired. Nina, you think it was awful, what I did, don't you?"

"Getting Jocelyn to marry you in that way?" The memory of old pain surged up in Nina, almost stifling her. "It hardly matters, does it? He couldn't have been much in love with me if he was so easy to get. I don't think he ever was, after the very beginning. I was just a habit. I don't think we'd ever got married."

She slipped on her dressing gown. She felt a sudden urgent desire to take a shower. She wanted to wash away something dark and noisome that had just washed over her, some feeling in herself compounded of bitterness, old jealousy, and dead anger.

"And it's a bit late in the day for worrying," she said, "and I'm a very forgiving type."

"Good night, then," Nicola said uneasily. She let herself out of the room.

Nina had a restless night. She could not make up her mind whether or not she was a forgiving type, or whether, in a quiet way, she had not just discovered that she hated Nicola. Not that Nina wanted Jocelyn now. Nicola was welcome to him. But to have been so uncomprehending, so deceived, such a fool, could still shock one's pride. And if hurt pride was not such a painful emotion as sheer grief, it was still a very wounding emotion. She thought it possible that once they were all

99

safely home in England, she might take pains never to see either of the Foleys again.

In the morning, when she went down the imposing staircase, she found Ruth sitting alone at the dining table, working her way through a very large helping of scrambled eggs and bacon. Used cups and plates on the table showed that the other Lyndons had already had breakfast. Ruth was in a close-fitting white trouser suit and had her golden hair loose about her shoulders. It made her look very pretty and very young. She looked up at Nina and said dutifully, "Merry Christmas!" though nothing could have been less merry than her tone. Then she got up, helped Nina to eggs, bacon, and tea from the sideboard, sat down again and went on eating. She seemed to be one of the people who prefer not to talk at breakfast. That suited Nina that morning.

But all of a sudden Ruth, raising her head, flicking her hair back with a nervous gesture of one hand, blurted out, "Bill says you're an actress."

"I try hard to be," Nina said, "but I haven't been getting anywhere much."

"Alison's an art student."

"I know."

"She's pretty good too. I think some day she'll be famous."

"That sounds fine."

"I'm the dud of the family."

"I don't expect you are."

"I am. I'm not good at anything. I'm not even good at getting married." Ruth flicked her hair away from her face again with a gesture that was like a nervous twitch. "I simply won't be married on the rebound."

"That sounds very sensible." Nina wondered why the girl

made her feel ten years older than she was. "But are you sure that's all it is."

"Of course it is," Ruth replied. "Ern was crazy about Alison. He didn't know I existed. But as soon as she went away he started following me around, and now he wants us to get married. But I think it's only some sort of defiance. He wants to show Alison he can do quite nicely without her." Ruth got up and helped herself to more bacon and eggs. She was young enough to be able to consume great quantities of food while remaining as slim as a reed. "Of course, I've always been in love with him and he's always known it. I've never pretended I wasn't. I'm not clever at pretending. I'm not clever at anything. But I don't want to marry him if the person he really wants is Alison."

"Don't you think he's had time to recover from her?"

"It's only a year."

"That's quite a time, even if it was a bad blow. And perhaps it wasn't. Being in love with someone who doesn't care for you can be a bit unrewarding. You're liable to grow out of it sooner or later. Because I suppose Alison never did care for him much."

"Alison's never cared about anybody. She lives for her art." Ruth said it with a solemn sort of respect.

Bill came into the room as she spoke.

"Not Alison," he said. "She lives for Alison."

"What about her baby?" Ruth said. "She won't give it up. So she must care for it a bit."

"For the moment, but she'll get tired of it. Merry Christmas, Nina."

She answered, "Merry Christmas."

"Does the idea of a short guided tour of the winery appeal to you at all?" he asked. "It's not too hot yet for a short walk there and back, and there'll be no crowds today, winetasting, as it's shut up because of Christmas."

"I'd like it very much," Nina said.

She finished her tea and went out into the garden with him.

They went down the drive, under the pines that stood up very straight and alone in the flat countryside. The dogs followed them, prancing at their heels. Just before reaching the end of the avenue Bill turned aside and opened a gate in a wire fence. As they passed through it Nina saw a low stone building ahead of them. It was half-smothered in vines, with the peak of a corrugated iron roof showing above them. There were rosebeds around it and a fine cedar near the entrance. It had a sort of homeliness about it, a pleasant charm.

"You understand, this is quite a small show," Bill said as they walked towards the building. "There are fewer and fewer of these places left. They're all getting bought up by the big combines. But I don't think we'll ever sell out unless we're driven to it. When my grandfather came out here, the place was all mallee. He used to tell me about it. They came by wagon, through dust storms. It was his father who got a block of land and started to clear it. And he'd just about got things going when there was a three-year drought. After that the rabbits came and destroyed everything. He had to start over and over again. There was no irrigation, of course, and no transport but the river. And just when a good harvest was ripening, the river suddenly dried up and everything was lost. There weren't any locks then to control that sort of thing. Floods were another trouble. When my grandfather finally built himself his fine house, as he thought it, he put it on the only hill in the place, because of the risk of floods. Then when everything seemed to be going well at last, there was the worst heat wave we've ever had. The temperature went up to a hundred and twenty-two and my father says he can remember the smell of the grapes cooking on the vines."

Bill took keys out of his pocket, unlocked a door and pushed it open. He and Nina went through it and he shut it again to keep the dogs out.

Inside it was dark until he switched on some lights. There was an overpowering wine smell. The lights shone on stone walls, painted white, on a table with a row of bottles and glasses on it, ready for winetasting, on long avenues of casks. Near to the door there were two enormous casks that reached almost to the ceiling, with cobwebs draping the space between them and the rafters. Round the middle of one of them someone had written in chalk, "1966–19, 1967–11, 1968–14," and so on up to the present time, with varying numbers. Nina asked what it meant and Bill told her that it was a record of the number of snakes caught in the building each year. She asked if the snakes were poisonous and he answered, "You bet!" Pipes, coiled like snakes, lay along the floor, used, he explained, for pumping wine from the tanks into the casks. He led the way along one of the passageways between the casks and showed Nina the tanks below the planks on which they were standing, full of liquid darkness, in the depths of which she could see her own face pallidly reflected.

"Interested?" Bill asked.

"Very," she answered. "And you're very proud of it, aren't you?—of all that your family's achieved."

"Wouldn't you be?"

"Yes."

"But I expect you think that house of ours is fantastic," he said. "It's only about eighty years old, yet we treat it as if it's historical, preserving everything, even what's hideous."

"If you go on doing that for long enough," Nina said, "it'll become historical."

"All the same, to a European, it must seem rather funny. But think of the vast distances the timber for that frightful staircase had to be brought, and the marble for the fireplaces, and all the furniture being shipped out from England. Think of what that meant in terms of success to people who'd begun with nothing. Think of the pride that went into doing it. We all love our home."

"But why did you have to roof it with corrugated iron?" she asked. "Wouldn't your pride have run to a few tiles?"

"Corrugated iron is the great Australian contribution to architecture." Bill grinned. "Perhaps you think we should roof our houses with our T-bone steaks and eat our roofs and fences. You found that steak last night pretty hard going, didn't you? You know, most of the beef we produce gets sold to America as hamburger. We haven't got your lush pastures. But you'll find our turkey all right. Also you'll find Christmas here is quite different from in Europe. It isn't simply the temperature, it's that here it's just a holiday. In Europe it's a festival."

"You seem to know quite a lot about Europe," Nina said. "Have you spent much time there?"

"I spent three years at Cambridge," he said. "It may surprise you, but I was a Rhodes scholar."

"I'm not exactly surprised," she said, "though you rather like to play that side of yourself down."

"That's just Australian. We hate to admit we're anything but tough eggs."

"And you like to knock Australia, don't you?"

"Another Australian habit. But a strictly Australian privilege too. It would be very tactless to try agreeing with us."

"Oh, I realise that. What was your subject?"

"Biochemistry. But I never meant to do anything in the

end but what I'm doing now. I never had any doubts about it."

"How marvellous not to have doubts. I have nothing else. I shouldn't feel myself without them."

"Then keep them, because I like you very much as you are."

Gently he put his hands on her shoulders, turned her towards him and laid his mouth on hers.

It was very quiet among the tall casks of wine. There was an almost cloistered solemnity about it. Then as Bill's arms moved from her shoulders down her arms, drawing her closer to him, the dogs, who had pushed their way in through the door that after all had not been quite closed, leapt up to get between them, barking in furious jealousy.

"Oh, damn the bloody brutes!" Bill exclaimed, letting go of Nina and aiming a kick that missed the yelping poodle. "They're too bloody human. They enjoy spoiling things."

He and Nina were both laughing as they walked out into the sunshine.

When they reached the house they found that champagne had been brought out on to the verandah. An immense meal of turkey and plum pudding followed. They drank a good deal of a Lyndon Hermitage with it, then they returned to the verandah in a state of bloated contentment, and coffee was brought out. Winnie Lyndon almost at once went comfortably to sleep in her chair. Her husband nodded. It was Ern Wilding, appearing round a corner of the house, who suggested that they should all go swimming.

The elder Lyndons declined, but everyone else agreed to go down to the river. They changed into what the Lyndons called their bathers in the house. Nina had a blue swimsuit and a scarlet, thigh-length terry wrap. Nicola's swimsuit was yellow and her wrap was a riot of yellow and orange flowers.

"Are you going to swim?" Nina asked her, remembering Nicola's fear of the Murray, as they followed the others towards the trees at the bottom of the garden. They could see the glint of water through them.

"I'll see," Nicola answered. Her tone was listless and she was walking slowly.

Jocelyn, ahead of them, walking with Ern Wilding, paused and waited for them. Like Nina, he asked Nicola, "Are you going to swim?"

She said again, "I'll see."

"You could just sit in the sun, if you'd prefer that," he said.

"Yes."

"All the same, a swim might do you good."

"Yes, it might."

"It might freshen you up."

"Yes, perhaps."

"But not if you don't feel like it."

"No." She could not be reached. The resignation with which she spoke was a defence that could not be penetrated.

Jocelyn glanced across her at Nina with a look of exasperation, then strode ahead again, swinging his towel, the laces of his corduroy shoes, which he had not bothered to tie, flapping as he walked. His skin was now a wholesome shade of chestnut, yet he looked nervously tense and not at all relaxed.

They emerged through the belt of trees onto a path that led along the riverside. The path was near the edge of a low cliff of red-brown rock that sloped down steeply into the opaque, olive-green water. The cliff did not extend far. Soon the path led downwards to a bank only just above the level of the river. The path was shaded by gums with papery-looking bark that peeled away in long strips, leaving the pale wood of the tree trunks bare. More trees, all with their roots in the water and all of them dead, lined both sides of the river. They were only the skeletons of trees, the dry white bones of them. There was something macabre about them. The place was a kind of cemetery, in spite of the way the sunshine glinted on the green ripples.

Adrian explained to Nina and Nicola that the trees had died when a series of locks built along the river had altered its level. Nicola gave a slight shudder, looking at them thoughtfully, as if she found something ominous about the serried ranks of corpses.

A little farther on there was a curve in the riverbank where there was a band of pebbles, making a little beach from which it was easy to wade out into the water. It had a wonderfully cool, silken feeling. Nicola did not go into it. She sat down on the pebbles with her knees drawn up to her chin and her arms wrapped round them, gazing away upstream as if something about the graveyard of trees had cast a spell on her. Presently, before the others had come out of the water, she got up and strolled away up the path towards the house.

It was about half past five when they all made their way back to it. The day's celebrations, the champagne in the morning, the turkey and plum pudding, the sunshine and the swimming were affecting them all in the same way. Everyone was yawning. Everyone was sleepy. One by one they wandered off to their rooms, told by Ruth that they had plenty of time to lie down if they wanted to before the late cold supper that was all they could expect that evening.

"Give me your bathers," she said to Nina and the others, "and I'll hang them up to dry."

Nina stripped off her damp wrap and swimsuit, tossed them out of her door, wrapped herself in her dressing gown, lay down on her bed, and by the time that she had settled herself comfortably was fast asleep.

She was wakened she had no idea how much later to a sense of stark fear and with her heart thumping wildly. It was the abruptness of that waking out of the depths of a dreamless sleep that brought the feeling of terror. Someone shouting had wakened her. Yet at first she did not take in what the voice was crying out. Then she recognized it as Ruth's and realised that she was yelling, "Bill! Bill!"

From the sound of it, she was at the bottom of the stairs.

"Bill!" she screamed. "There's someone in the river! Bill—come quick! Ern's there, but he can't manage alone. Bill!"

Nina shot to the door. As she opened it, Ruth came running up the stairs and dashed into her brother's room. He was sitting on the edge of his bed, pulling on his shoes, and swearing while he did it. Then he thrust past Ruth in the doorway and went running down the stairs.

Nina caught at Ruth's arm as she turned to follow him.

"Ruth, is she dead?"

Ruth did not answer, but raced after Bill.

The dogs, both asleep on the verandah, woke, uttered a drowsy bark or two, then suddenly realising that there was something exciting afoot, went racing after Ruth.

Nina turned back into her room, pulled on the first clothes that came to hand, ran down the stairs and out across the lawn towards the belt of trees. Bill and Ruth had disappeared among them already. Nina followed the path through them, emerging at the top of the red cliff.

That was as far as she had to go.

Down below the cliff Ern Wilding was in the water, trying to dislodge a limp shape from something that held it fast below the surface of the water. Bill was swimming towards him from the beach from which they had all bathed that afternoon. Ruth was on the cliff, on her knees at the edge of it, calling out to Bill to hurry.

But there was no need to hurry. When Ern and Bill between them managed to set Jocelyn loose from the grip of some underwater tree root, it was obvious that he was dead. He was one with all those stark white trees that stood motionless and waiting along the banks of the river.

Carefully the two men towed his clumsily lolling body to the beach and lifted it out onto the pebbles.

Chapter Nine

Jocelyn was wearing his swimming trunks and corduroy shoes. One shoelace was undone, the other was missing. That held Nina's attention in the way that an insignificant detail will at a time of crisis. She found herself remembering that Jocelyn had hardly ever troubled to tie the laces of those shoes when he wore them to go down to the beach at Glenelg, and there was a curious kind of sadness in the thought that even in such small ways you can go on being yourself and not somehow be dramatically changed up to the very moment when death strikes.

Jocelyn's towel was near to where she was still standing on the cliff above the place where his body had been held by the sunken tree. She bent unthinkingly to pick the towel up. But then she straightened up again, leaving it where it was, and walked slowly on until she stood beside him.

Rapid footsteps behind her made her look round. Winnie and Henry Lyndon were coming quickly along the path. Bill and Ern, in their clinging wet clothes, and Ruth who had gone ahead of Nina to the little beach, all stood back to let the older couple see what was there on the ground.

They greeted the sight at first in horrified silence.

Then in a low voice Henry Lyndon said, "We heard Ruth shouting. How did it happen?"

For a moment no one answered. The dogs, held back by Bill, made frightened little whining noises.

"Ern found him," Ruth said.

"A doctor!" Winnie exclaimed, her voice grating but tightly controlled. "Ruth, go and telephone—"

"Wait," her husband said. "A doctor isn't going to be able to do anything for him. Tell me what happened, Ern, then I'll phone the police station."

"I just came down here," Ern said, passing his hand nervously over his damp face. "I don't know why. I just came for a stroll. And there he was, tangled up with that stump down there." He pointed at the place. "I swam along to him, but I couldn't get him loose, so Ruth ran back to the house to get Bill and we got him out between us."

"You and Ruth came down for this stroll together, did you?" Henry asked.

Ern and Ruth glanced at one another. It was an almost conspiratorial glance, as if they were agreeing together how to answer this.

"Well, no," Ern said. "I came on my own. Ruth was a bit behind me."

"We'd had a row," Ruth said in a sudden rush of words, "and Ern went walking off in a rage, and I was going to let him go, and then I thought, 'Well, it's Christmas, it's the wrong sort of day to quarrel,' so I followed him down here to make peace and there he was in the river, holding on to Jocelyn and shouting at me to go back to the house to get Bill."

"Yes, I see," her father said. "But you didn't see Jocelyn come down, Ern? You didn't see how he fell in?"

Ern shook his head.

"Why d'you say fell in?" Winnie asked. "You know how easy it is to get a cramp here if you get caught in one of the cold currents. And Jocelyn didn't know this river, how unsafe it is to go swimming alone."

"You don't usually go swimming in your shoes," Henry said.

Nina spoke abruptly. "Someone's got to tell Nicola."

"Yes," Bill said.

"I'll go—"

But as she said it, Adrian and Brenda appeared together on the path above them. They both stood there for a moment, then Adrian came loping forward at a shambling run. Brenda hesitated, as if really she wanted to turn away quickly from the sight of death, but then she came after Adrian. It was she who asked what had happened.

Before anyone could answer, Adrian cried, "He's dead, isn't he? He's dead?"

Brenda put a hand on his arm, holding it firmly. "You can see that. What happened, Mr. Lyndon?"

He told her what Ern and Ruth had just told him.

"And someone's got to tell Nicola," Nina said again.

"Let's go together," Brenda said.

"I was just wondering, what's happened to Nicola?" Bill said. "The rest of us heard Ruth shouting and came down. Adrian, that's why you and Brenda came down, wasn't it? You heard Ruth."

Adrian did not seem to hear him. He was staring down at Jocelyn with shocked, uncomprehending eyes.

Brenda answered for him. "Yes, we'd both been asleep, but Ruth woke us. We didn't know what was wrong, but we saw you all streaming down here, so we got up and dressed and came to see if we could help. But we never dreamt of finding Jocelyn. . . ."

"Yet Nicola didn't hear Ruth," Bill said. "Or if she did,

she didn't think of coming, though she'd have seen that Jocelyn wasn't in their room."

"I don't know what you're suggesting," Nina said. "Why should she jump to the conclusion Jocelyn was dead simply because he wasn't in their room? He could have gone for a walk, like Ern, or anything. She may even be asleep still and never heard Ruth at all. I'm going up to her now."

"Would you like me to come with you?" Brenda asked.

"Yes, will you? I expect it'll be easier if we do it together."

"All right, let's go."

Nina and Brenda started back along the path to the house. As soon as they were out of earshot of the others, Brenda said rapidly, "Nina, it's an awful thought, but d'you think Jocelyn could have gone down there and thrown himself in the river? What d'you think? Could he?"

"I don't know, I don't know," Nina answered. "It's no good guessing."

"He was pretty near breaking point, I know," Brenda said, "because he's talked about it a good deal to Adrian. And whatever you say, there's something queer about Nicola not coming down. Ruth woke me up, shouting, and I was quite sound asleep. Were you asleep too?"

"Yes."

"Yet she didn't waken Nicola. What I was thinking is, suppose she and Jocelyn had a row of some sort. . . . Oh God, why did I ever agree to come here? I thought it would do her good, but we ought to have stayed at home. It's my fault. I always do the wrong thing. I'm always going to blame myself."

They entered the house.

It was as silent as if it were empty. Mrs. Bollard, the housekeeper, had gone to spend the afternoon with her family in Mildura and everyone else except Nicola was down by the river.

Brenda started for the stairs. But suddenly she hung back, more nervous than Nina would have expected her to be, and let Nina go ahead of her.

"I'm scared," Brenda whispered. "I'm dead scared of trying to tell her about Jocelyn. I'm no good at that sort of thing. I blurt out the first thing that comes into my head. You'll do it far better than I shall."

Nina was scared herself. But what she feared most was that on hearing of Jocelyn's death, Nicola might smile at her. Nina could visualize that smile with uncanny exactitude. It would be a slightly mad and brilliantly carefree smile. The smile of reprieve.

Reaching the room shared by Jocelyn and Nicola, Nina opened the door.

There was no one there.

Brenda, following Nina into the room, looked round and said, "What's happened to her?"

"Gone downstairs, I suppose," Nina said. "We'll have to look for her."

Brenda advanced further into the room.

"You know, it doesn't look as if either of them lay down like the rest of us," she said, "unless they straightened their beds up very carefully afterwards."

Nina nodded. The counterpanes on both beds were as smooth as if the beds had just been made.

She and Brenda went downstairs again.

They went from room to room, but all were empty. They went out on to the verandah and called out Nicola's name, in case she were somewhere in the garden. There was no answer.

"She must have gone for a walk," Brenda said. "What shall we do? I suppose we'll just have to wait for her."

"It doesn't sound very like Nicola to go for a walk in this heat," Nina said. "And which way could she have gone?"

"There's the drive. Shall we go along it and see? Or shall we just wait? I think it would probably be best to wait, or we may miss her altogether."

A disturbing thought had begun to nag at Nina's mind.

"I know one thing I want to do," she said. "I'm going to take a look in the garage."

"The garage? Why the garage? Oh—" Brenda's hand went to her mouth. "You aren't thinking of that carbon monoxide thing!"

"I was thinking she may have wanted to get away," Nina answered.

"But even if she did, how could she?"

"She can drive."

"But she hasn't got a car."

"All the same, let's go and see."

Brenda gave an uneasy wriggle of her shoulders, but followed Nina to the garage.

They reached it through the kitchen. The garage jutted out from the side of the house near to the back door. In the yard that they had to cross to the garage entrance their bathers had been pegged up on a line to dry. They were a disconcertingly gay reminder of a time that had already begun to seem a long while ago. The garage doors were open. Nina and Brenda went in.

The Foleys' Holden was missing.

Brenda's face became a dead blank for a moment, then anger brought it back to life.

"Of all the nerve!" She stared at the empty space where

the Holden had stood. "But how, Nina? I'm sure we didn't leave the keys in the car."

"Perhaps you did, just for once," Nina said.

"No, we *never* do!"

"Where do you keep them normally?"

"We've each got a set. I keep mine in my handbag."

"Where's your handbag?"

"In our room. But d'you really think she'd go into our room and steal something out of my handbag?"

"She seems to have stolen your car."

"Yes, and I suppose she could have got the keys when she came back here from the river, while we were still in swimming."

"You didn't look in your handbag after you got in?"

"No, why should I?" Brenda turned back towards the kitchen door. "But let's go and make sure."

In the house, as they went to the foot of the stairs, they heard a voice coming from a room that opened off the central passage. Henry Lyndon was talking on the telephone to someone called Grable. Whether he was a doctor or a policeman was not clear, but Henry was asking him to come as quickly as possible.

Nina and Brenda went upstairs and into the room shared by Brenda and Adrian. Her handbag lay on the dressing table. She opened the bag and searched through it.

"You're right," she said, "they've gone." She looked at Nina, frowning. "Where will she head for?"

"Just off into the blue somewhere, I should think," Nina said. "Anywhere away from Jocelyn. She talked to me about that the other evening."

"D'you think she'll try to get home?"

"She hasn't much money. Only some jewellery she talked of selling. Let's go and see if the things are still in her room, or if she's taken them. If they're still there, it probably means she means to come back once she's driven around the country for a bit and got something out of her system."

But the jewellery was gone. So were Nicola's clothes, her handbag, and a suitcase.

Nina and Brenda stood in the middle of the room, looking at one another, silent.

Suddenly Nina went to the chest of drawers and reopened a drawer into which she had already looked. It contained some of Jocelyn's belongings, some socks, some handkerchiefs, and also his wallet. She took it out and opened it. Jocelyn's passport and airline ticket were there, but Nicola's were gone, and except for his traveller's cheques, all signed with his name and so no use to Nicola, there was no money.

Brenda was watching her.

"You shouldn't have done that," she said. "The police always say one mustn't touch anything."

"Anyway, now we know," Nina said. She put the wallet back into the drawer and closed it. "She's got Jocelyn's loose cash, her passport and ticket, and her jewellery. And that means she's heading for home. And if Jocelyn hadn't happened to get drowned, no one would have any right to stop her."

"Except that she's stolen our car."

"That's all in the family. I suppose she's driving back to Adelaide."

"Unless she's going to Melbourne," Brenda said. "That would really be better, if she's trying to get home. She could fly direct from there. From Adelaide she'd have to change planes. But she may not know that. And she'll never get there, Nina. Even if she doesn't collapse and wreck the car, they'll stop her because—because this means she pushed Jocelyn into the river, doesn't it? *Doesn't it?*" Her own ques-

117

tion seemed to shock her and she clapped her hand over her mouth again, as if, too late she wanted to shut in the words. Then, letting her hand fall, she gave a shaky sigh. "I don't know what I'm saying. Perhaps she didn't even know that he was dead."

"Yes, she could have gone before we got back from our swim."

"But Jocelyn would have wondered where she was and noticed her things were missing. He'd have raised the alarm."

"He might not have wanted to. He might have wandered down to the river, trying to think things out. You said yourself he was pretty near to breaking point. He may have thought it might be best to let her go away."

"And fallen into the river in a fit of absentmindedness?" Brenda's voice went harsh. "No, Nina, I think I'll stick to what I just said. I think Jocelyn and Nicola went down there to the river together and—well, it may not have been planned, but suddenly there was a moment when it was easy and she pushed him in. That's what she believed he'd done to her twice, wasn't it? Seized an opportunity and pushed. It was nonsense, of course, but she believed it. And when she'd done it, she panicked and bolted."

"But she must have taken your car keys before we came back from the river."

"Yes, that's true. Well then, she had it planned. She meant to do it, if she had the chance. Perhaps it was she who suggested that they should go down to the river again."

"And it all happened without anyone seeing anything?"

"We were all asleep. Anyway, we don't know she wasn't seen by anyone. The police will be going into that. And there they are, I think." Men's voices from downstairs reached them through the open door. "We'd better go down and tell them about the car and everything."

Chapter Ten

They went downstairs to meet the policemen. There were two of them in uniform talking to Henry Lyndon. As Nina and Brenda came downstairs, they all looked up.

"Have you told her?" Henry asked. "How is she?"

"No, we haven't told her," Brenda replied. "We couldn't. She's gone."

"Gone? Gone where?"

"We don't know," she said. "But she wasn't anywhere in the house when we got here, then we found she'd taken my car keys and the Holden has vanished. Our guess is that she's on the way back to Adelaide, or else to Melbourne." Brenda sounded more like her normal self, taking charge of the situation, relieving Nina of the responsibility of answering questions. "We've taken a quick look round and she seems to have packed all her things, taken her ticket and passport, and gone."

"Is she out of her wits?" Henry asked.

"We're afraid perhaps, in a way, she is," Brenda answered.

He looked at her hard, then at Nina. Then it occurred to him that he should introduce them to the policemen and ask the men if they wanted to take a look round the house and garage for themselves.

The senior of the two policemen, Sergeant Grable, replied

that they would prefer to go down to the river first to take a look at the dead man.

"But we'd like to hear more about this when we get back, if the ladies will wait," he said. "And when Dr. Crabbe shows up here, perhaps they'd send him straight down to us."

The three men set off across the lawn to the river.

It was only a few minutes later that the doctor arrived. He was a short, clumsily built man of about fifty, with lumpy features and shrewd little eyes. He seemed irritated at having had his Christmas Day interrupted and walked off after the other men, muttering to himself in a rumbling grumble.

About ten minutes later Adrian and the others, with the exception of Henry Lyndon, returned to the house. Brenda and Nina had settled on the verandah. Dusk had come and the tip of Brenda's cigarette glowed bright. Adrian went to her, stood behind her, and put his hands on her shoulders, as if he were in desperate need of the touch of her. She put up a hand to cover one of his.

"They've told you about Nicola, have they?" she asked.

"Only that she's gone," he said. "That she took the car. That's all I know."

"That's all we know," she said.

"Bill, you and Ern had better go and change," Winnie Lyndon said. "You can find something for Ern to put on. You're both soaking."

"Don't worry, Mrs. Lyndon, I'll soon dry out," Ern said.

"Well, I'll go and see to some supper." She went into the house.

"We could do with some drinks," Bill said.

"I'll get them," Ruth said and turned to follow her mother indoors.

"Just a minute." Bill pushed his damp hair back from his forehead. "Something's puzzling me. That row you and Ern

120

had, Ruth, before he walked off to the river, where were you when you had it?"

"Here on the verandah," Ruth said. "We came down when we'd changed and sat and talked. And then we started arguing, and then we started quarrelling. Now I'll get those drinks. I've never wanted one so badly."

"Hold on," Bill said. "If you were here, why didn't you see Jocelyn go down to the river?"

"Playing amateur detectives, Bill?" She gave a dry little laugh. "I'd leave it to the professionals. And it's obvious, Jocelyn must have gone by the path." She gestured towards the high bank of flowering shrubs to the left of the lawn. "If he'd gone that way, we shouldn't have seen him. And he knew the path was there. I know he did, because I remember coming on him there on that other visit of his, and the reason I remember it is that he was kissing Alison. And Alison was kissing him back, my word, she was! And I was quite a bit shocked, if you want to know, because I thought she was supposed to be in love with Ern and I thought Jocelyn had a girl in England, and I took kisses very, very seriously in those days." Her voice had taken on a childishly dramatized bitterness. She went indoors.

"Don't take any notice of her," Ern said, shifting uneasily from one foot to the other. His damp cotton trousers clung to his long legs. "She's got this thing about Alison at the moment, because of this news that Bill brought back, but she'll grow out of it."

"But she could be right about Jocelyn going down to the river that way," Bill said.

"Why should he do that?" Ern asked.

"He may have heard you and Ruth on the verandah—if you were having a row, your voices may have risen a bit, I dare say—and he didn't want to interrupt you."

Ern nodded. "Yes, it could have been like that."

Adrian had drawn a chair close to Brenda's. He sat down and took one of her hands. For an instant she looked impatient, as if for once she found something unsatisfying in his dependence on her, but then with her free hand she touched his cheek gently and at that touch of sympathy his eyes suddenly overflowed and tears went rolling down his cheeks. Taking his glasses off, he mopped at the tears, then blew on the glasses and polished them and put them on again, as if they were armour against his own emotions. He looked tolerably composed by the time that Ruth came out, carrying a tray of drinks.

Several more men arrived at the house soon afterwards. Two of them were detectives in plain clothes, one was a photographer, two were men with a stretcher. Bill accompanied them to the riverbank, but in a few minutes he returned, together with his father.

"They're not satisfied about things," Henry Lyndon said. "Seems there are one or two peculiar things about the situation. For instance, Crabbe says, it's clear Jocelyn had a heavy blow on the side of his head. It's true he may have got that hitting that sunken tree in the river, or on some rock on the way down, but it's something they aren't happy about. They'll be able to tell more probably when Crabbe's done the autopsy. He says he'll be doing it tonight. At the moment they don't even know if it was the blow that killed him, or if he died by drowning."

Brenda had slid her hand out of Adrian's to light another cigarette.

"Why aren't they looking for Nicola?" she demanded. "That's what they ought to be doing."

"Give them a little time," Henry said. "They haven't had long."

"Where will they take him?" Adrian asked anxiously. "Where will they do this autopsy?"

"I'm afraid we don't run to a mortuary in Elderwood," Henry replied. "They'll probably put him in the cold room at the hotel."

"The *hotel!*" Adrian said in a shocked croak, as if there were irreverence in the thought.

"I'm afraid it's the best we can do here," Henry said.

"That reminds me," Brenda said. "We'll move to the hotel tomorrow, Mr. Lyndon. We can't go on involving you in our troubles."

"Now isn't that absurd?" Winnie Lyndon said, coming out onto the verandah and dropping into one of the basket chairs, her short skirt going sliding up her legs. "Of course you'll stay here as long as you need to."

"But that's imposing on you terribly," Brenda said. "We can't, we really can't."

"You can, lovey, and you will," Winnie responded, "so don't worry."

"And after all," Bill said, "we're involved ourselves. It happened here."

His words, or perhaps the tone in which he spoke them, produced a brief silence.

Ruth broke it jerkily. "All this talking! Why don't you give us more drinks, Bill?"

He was moving towards the table where she had put the tray down when a figure emerged from the trees and came through the twilight towards them.

It was one of the detectives, Sergeant Furness, a tall, fleshy man with greying hair and a round, unexpressive slab of a face. He was wearing a light grey suit, a mauve shirt, and a highly coloured tie, in which he looked far more as if he had come to a party than to investigate a death. Probably his clothes were what he had put on for his Christmas festivities.

"Can I use your telephone, Mr. Lyndon?" he said. "I want to get a call out for Mrs. Foley. And then I'd like to talk to the lady who found she was missing."

"We found it together, Miss Hemslow and I," Brenda replied. "I'm Mrs. Foley's sister-in-law. Miss Hemslow is a friend of hers."

"Right, Mrs. Foley," Sergeant Furness said. "I'd like to talk to you in a minute, but first I'd like to telephone."

He was a few minutes on the telephone, then he reappeared and asked if there were some room that he could use for asking a few questions. He had been joined by then by the second detective. Henry took them into the house, beckoning Brenda to follow. She gave Adrian's shoulder a little pat before she went, as if to keep him calm while she was gone, and about a quarter of an hour later returned and told Nina that she was wanted by the sergeant.

He was in a small room furnished as an office. There were steel filing cabinets, a big desk, a swivel chair, a table with a typewriter on it, a telephone, a tape recorder. This room was probably the vital centre of the house, the core of the activity on which all the rest depended.

Sergeant Furness had taken the swivel chair at the desk. The other detective was standing by the window. The sergeant sat sideways at the desk, one elbow resting on it, one leg crossed over the other. He had a ballpoint pen in his hand, with which he tapped his teeth.

He asked for Nina's full name and her home address and made a note of them.

"Mrs. Foley's told me how you and she found her sister-in-law gone," he went on, "but I'd like to hear it from you, if you don't mind. May be details she's forgotten, that sort

124

of thing. You're both very worried at the way your friend's cleared out, I imagine."

"Wouldn't you be?" Nina said.

"That's for sure. Specially in the circumstances."

"The circumstances being that her husband's been found dead."

"Right. Makes it awkward, doesn't it? But don't worry, we'll find her soon. There aren't many roads she could have taken. Though if she got off on to side roads she could easily get lost. We'll hope she didn't do that. D'you know, in the kind of country we've got round here, you get cases every so often of people, strangers mostly, who get lost in the bush and actually die of thirst when they're only a mile or two from one of the main roads."

Nina began to think that her interview with the sergeant was not going to cheer her in any way.

"Just what do you want to know?" she asked.

"What you did when you came to the house to break the news about Mr. Foley's death," he said.

She told him what she and Brenda had done and he listened without interrupting, absentmindedly tapping his teeth until she described how she had looked in Jocelyn's wallet.

At that point, with uncontrollable exasperation, he broke in, "There, it's what I always say, they *will* do it! They will go rummaging around, messing up the evidence, before the poor coppers have a chance. You shouldn't have touched anything, don't you know that?"

"I suppose I did, only I was so worried," Nina said.

"Everyone's always so worried they can't leave anything alone. Always. They know they're not supposed to touch anything but they just can't keep their fingers out of it. Find a dead body, what do they do? Turn it over, move it around, trample all around the place. Never, never leave everything just the way it is, so the coppers have a chance."

"They couldn't have left Jocelyn where he was," Nina said. "He might have been alive."

"Right," he agreed, but he sounded grudging about it. "I'm not arguing, I'm just telling you one of the facts of life. Now tell me why you were so worried you were ready to risk mucking up what might be important evidence."

"Well, the trouble was," Nina said, "she's recently developed an extraordinary fear of her husband and I knew she wanted to get away from him. She talked to me about it a day or two ago. So that's what I thought of as soon as we found she was missing and the car gone too. I thought she was trying to vanish. So I checked up on the passport and ticket to find out what she was trying to do, go home or somehow drop out of sight here in Australia. And then I wanted to think out what I ought to do about it."

"Did you have any ideas about what you ought to do?" Sergeant Furness asked.

She shook her head. "What *could* I do, except tell you all about it, because you're the only people who can stop her doing herself some harm?"

"Right," he said. "Now this fear of her husband you mentioned, what was at the back of that?"

"Probably nothing. But she'd convinced herself that he was trying to kill her."

"And was he?" The sergeant's voice was matter-of-fact, as if he heard such statements every day of his life.

"I don't know," Nina answered.

"You don't feel sure he wasn't?"

"I don't know."

"You think it's just possible he might have been."

"I honestly don't know."

126

"Interesting, all the same, that you aren't certain. People usually are about a thing like that, even when they're wrong. You've no opinions even on the subject?"

"I didn't think it was likely."

"Didn't—past tense," he said. "Any difference in your feelings now?"

"Because he's dead himself? I don't see that that tells one anything."

"Maybe it doesn't. Maybe it wouldn't tell his wife anything either. But if it was in her mind that he was trying to kill her, that was reason enough for her to give him a smart push into the river."

"You don't believe that!" The fact that, ever since Brenda had suggested it, this fear had been in the forefront of Nina's mind only made her protest the more emphatic.

"Open mind," he answered. "That's what I'm trying to keep at the moment. Always a difficult thing to do, but you can train yourself in it up to a point. Now tell me how he's supposed to have tried to kill her."

"Well, do you know about her baby being stolen?" Nina asked.

He nodded. "The other Mrs. Foley told me. About the cruellest thing you can do to a woman, I'd say, and to a man too, if he's the kind who cares about his kids. No wonder she hadn't been thinking straight lately."

"Yes. Then, you see, she got it into her head that her husband blamed her for what had happened and hated her because of it. So when he tripped on the edge of a pavement in Mexico City and fell against her, so that she nearly went under a lorry, and when she fell off a cable car in Wellington and nearly went under another one, she thought both times he'd done it on purpose. Then there was a time before they left home when she believed he'd tried to poison her with barbiturates, but lost his nerve and thrown the stuff away. And there was another time—but she said that never happened. I don't know whether it did or not. It was her husband who told me about it. He said she shut herself in the garage and tried to kill herself with carbon monoxide and that he got her out only just in time."

"Did you believe him or her about that?"

"I really don't know. Nicola said that his having told me the story meant that that was what was going to happen when they got home, that he was sort of preparing me for the idea of her suicide in that way."

"Since none of the other attempts on her life had been successful. After all, you can't go on having an unlimited number of near-fatal accidents all over the world, can you? Sooner or later someone curious, like me, is bound to start asking questions."

"But I didn't say they *were* attempts on her life."

"No, no, nor did you."

"I only said she thought they were."

"Right. Nothing to show they weren't, all the same. You probably don't believe people really do that sort of thing, but they do, you know, all the time. Mustn't ever forget that. Now tell me, will you, what were you doing yourself when Mr. Foley was falling into the river and Mrs. Foley was stealing her brother-in-law's car and driving off we don't know where?"

"Just when did Jocelyn fall in?"

"Not so very long before he was found, or there'd have been yabbies sticking to him."

"Yabbies?"

"Small fresh-water crayfish. A delicacy. What were you doing?"

Nina remembered the crayfish at dinner the night before and nearly retched.

"I was sleeping," she answered.

"Sleeping," he said gloomily. "Like Mrs. Brenda Foley and her husband too, she says. And like everyone else in the house, I'll bet. My word, if you want to commit a crime, my advice is, do it in the afternoon of Christmas Day. Everyone's had too much to eat and drink, and it's hot, and they'll have been swimming, if they've had the chance, so what do they want to do but sleep, and who's going to see anything? You really didn't hear or see anything?"

"Nothing at all," Nina said. "I lay down as soon as I got to my room and fell fast asleep, and I didn't wake up till I heard Ruth Lyndon calling out about someone being in the river. But she and Mr. Wilding weren't asleep, they were out on the verandah."

"That's something, then. Thank you, Miss Hemslow."

"Is that all you want?"

"Unless there's anything else you can tell me."

"I don't think so." She stood up. "You said a crime, Mr. Furness. Have you made up your mind it's a crime and not an accident?"

"Well, that path down there is a pretty broad one to fall off by accident," he answered, "but of course it isn't impossible. The heat might have been too much for Mr. Foley. He wasn't accustomed to it. He could have got dizzy. Anything could have happened. I've still got that open mind I mentioned. Now if you'd be good enough to ask Mr. Wilding to come along and see me, I'd be grateful."

Sure that the sergeant was in fact convinced that Jocelyn's death was murder and that everything that she had said had helped to make him assume that Nicola was guilty, Nina went back to the silent group on the verandah and told them that the sergeant wanted to see Ern.

She was feeling too restless to sit down with the others, and hearing a clatter of dishes coming from the kitchen, she went to it and found Winnie there, carving up the remains of the cold turkey.

"Can I help?" Nina asked.

"Thanks, lovey, but there's nothing to do," Winnie said. "I've set the table already, and I'm only giving them some cold turkey and ham and salad. Oh, you could wash that lettuce, if you would. I know how you feel, you want to be doing something. That's what I'm like myself. When anything bad happens, I can't keep still. I have to keep moving around. Tell me, how did you make out with Ed Furness? We know him quite well, naturally, in a place like this, and we've always thought him a good man, but I don't know how he'll handle a terrible thing like this."

Nina went to the sink, turned on the cold tap and started to wash the lettuce under it.

"He thinks it's murder," she said, "and that Nicola did it."

"No!" Winnie let the carving knife and fork fall with a clatter onto the table. "The idea of it! Murder! I must talk to that man."

"You think it was an accident?" Nina said.

"Of course it was an accident. A terrible accident—terrible. But not murder."

"He said the path down there was a bit broad for anyone to have slipped off by accident."

"And is that all the evidence he's got? What nonsense. Of course that's what happened. I can even guess how and I shall tell him so. Didn't you notice Jocelyn's shoelaces, Nina? One was undone, the other was actually missing. It looks as if he'd a habit of not troubling to tie his laces. A bad habit, because there's nothing easier than to trip yourself up by stepping on a flapping shoelace. And that's what he did. Just stepped on the shoelace and tripped himself and fell into the river and hit his head against that sunken tree. If he hadn't hit his head, he wouldn't have died, poor soul, he'd have swum away to safety. Terrible, but not murder. The idea! I ask you—" She picked up the carving knife and brandished it. "I ask you, who is there here who'd even think of murder? Aren't we all decent, peaceable people? Don't we all know each other well? Oh, I know Jocelyn and Nicola were almost strangers, but haven't we known Jocelyn's brother and his wife for years? And you too, you're an old friend of Brenda's, and anyway, one's only got to look at you to know you're a nice normal girl. No, I'm going to talk to Ed and put him straight about a thing or two."

She turned to the door, still with the carving knife in her hand and not looking at all a peaceable person.

"He's talking to Ern at the moment," Nina said.

"Well, as soon as he's finished with Ern . . ." Winnie returned to her attack on the turkey. "And you say he thinks Nicola did it. You know, I liked her so much. If ever I saw a really gentle creature . . . Very sad and depressed, naturally, but quiet and sweet. And I don't believe for a moment she knew her husband was dead when she drove off. I think she just got in a bad mood for some reason, perhaps because it was Christmas, you know, and Christmas is the time for children, and she'd lost hers, and anyway, you're either very happy or very sad at Christmas, and she happened to be sad —so she went driving, and she'll come back presently. Lots of people find driving relaxes them when they get upset. Alison's like that. She always went driving if she was depressed about anything. I used to worry about it. I didn't think it was safe if her mind wasn't really on what she was

131

doing, but she never had an accident. She's a very good driver. Really, she's good at most things. And I don't care what anyone says, now that she's got a child, I'm sure she'll turn out a very good mother."

Nina realised that Winnie had not yet heard about the missing passport and ticket. Also that she would always use her formidable willpower to make sure that she never thought evil of anyone.

But her idea of how Jocelyn could have fallen into the river was a perfectly sound one. It was true that he had a habit of leaving his shoelaces undone when he went down to swim and that it is very easy to trip over a trailing shoelace. Nina felt gratitude for the suggestion.

"Now, lovey, if you'd just put that lettuce in this bowl, and slice up these tomatoes, it'd be a great help," Winnie said. "Then we can call the rest of them in for supper."

Chapter Eleven

Supper was an unsettled affair that evening. One by one everyone in the house was called away from the table by Sergeant Furness, whose questioning, however, was brief and, as each reported it to the others on returning to the cold turkey and ham, consisted of asking them where they had been from the time when they had returned from their swim until Ern's discovery of Jocelyn's body, and also whether or not anyone had seen him go down to the river.

With the exception of Ruth and Ern, who had been on the verandah, they had all told the sergeant that they had been asleep in their rooms, and Ruth and Ern had told him that they had not seen Jocelyn. So he must have gone down, they decided amongst themselves, by the path that ran behind the high bank of flowering shrubs to the left of the lawn, as Ruth had suggested earlier, choosing that way because he had not wanted to intrude on the quarrel going on, on the verandah.

Listening to the Lyndons' rather disconnected talking, Nina gathered that this path began close to the kitchen door and was virtually arched over by shrubs and trees. So if Jocelyn had gone that way, he would neither have been seen by Ruth and Ern, nor by anyone who might have been looking out of an upstairs window, just supposing that someone had not been telling the precise truth about being asleep. And Jocelyn would have reached the path by going through the kitchen, which, with the housekeeper away visiting her family and the daily help of course not there, would have been empty. Then, on reaching the riverbank, he had tripped over his shoelace. . . .

At first, when Winnie suggested to her family that that was how the accident had happened, she encountered a certain scepticism. But once she had stated her opinion often enough, doubt weakened, and the sheer relief of accepting her view began to show on all the faces round the table. Why Nicola had fled was still unexplained. But everyone knew, poor girl, that she had been in an unbalanced state. There need have been no rational cause for her action.

Nina, listening with strained attention, for some reason began to feel an intruder. All the others knew each other well, but she was a stranger, she did not belong here. And she felt somehow responsible for Nicola and Jocelyn and for their reprehensible actions, the one getting himself killed, to the great inconvenience of everyone, on Christmas Day of all days, and the other making things worse by driving off God knew where at a most inappropriate moment. Looking small and crushed in her chair at the big table, Nina felt as if she ought to have been able to prevent these things happening, and that the only reason she was not being told so by these people was that they were all so kind and nice. If she had been wiser, more perceptive, more patient, if she had tried harder, she could surely have smoothed out the troubles between Jocelyn and Nicola. Then everything would have turned out differently.

Not that making peace between them would necessarily have stopped Jocelyn tripping over his shoelace. . . .

Had she the faintest belief in that shoelace?

An immense weariness settled like a grey fog in Nina's brain. She could not think clearly. She could hardly peck at her food. But the meal dragged on, not because anyone else was eating much, but simply because no one had the resolution to get up and start clearing away. They sat round the table, drinking coffee and brandy, until Sergeant Furness had finished his questioning and had said good night and gone, along with the other policemen, and the darkness was pressing up outside the windows, showing them their own faces, reflected in the glass. Jocelyn's body had long since been taken away. They talked spasmodically and repeated themselves again and again, each reiteration reinforcing their conviction that his death was an accident. All except Bill, who was almost as silent as Nina.

When at last they got up and Nina had helped Ruth and Brenda clear the table and stack the dishes in the dishwasher, she went out to the verandah and sat down at the top of the steps leading down to the lawn. The others had wandered into the sitting room. She could hear their voices coming from it, still in little spurts of nervous talk. She wondered what they were planning to do about going to bed. Would they stay up half the night, on the chance that there might be some news of Nicola, or would they decide that enough was enough and go up to their rooms?

Nina sat with her elbows on her knees, her face between her hands, gazing into the depths of the darkness. Gradually it began to seem less dark. Shrubs and trees began to take shape against the sky. It was full of stars, with the Southern Cross low above the treetops. The Southern Cross had been a disappointment. She had imagined that it would be some great, dramatic cluster of stars, and instead it had turned out to be a rather small, rather pallid constellation, the only distinction of which seemed to be that you could not see it in the Northern Hemisphere. The evening was as hot as the day had been and near her she heard the ping of a mosquito. She slapped at it, missed, and heard it again. Then she heard footsteps coming along the verandah.

"You'll be eaten alive if you stay out here," Bill said.

"I like it here," she answered.

"You look as miserable as a bandicoot."

"What's that?" she asked. "Some fabulous animal?"

"You're mixing it up with the bandersnatch." He sat down beside her. "The bandicoot's a small animal we have in these parts, not quite as big as a rabbit. I used to have one as a pet when I was a kid. I fed it on tripe and cheese and potatoes."

"No wonder it was miserable."

"That's just an expression." He took hold of her chin and turned her face towards him. "If you want the truth, you look very, very miserable."

"You're not far wrong."

"I'm not full of wild joy myself."

"No." On an impulse she reached out to him and slid her arms round his neck. "Bill, help me, please. Hold me."

His arms went round her, holding her gently. After a moment he asked, "Does it help?"

"Very, very much. It's what I needed."

"Does it have to stop just there?"

"For now it does." She rested her head against his shoulder. "For this evening."

"I was afraid you'd say so." But he drew her a little closer.

"All I want is someone to hold on to," she said. "That's childish, isn't it? I'm sorry."

"But understandable—this evening."

"Please don't go away yet."

"It hadn't crossed my mind."

"Bill—" She lifted her head and gazed into his face, indistinct in the darkness. "Do you think it *was* an accident this afternoon? I was watching you in there and I didn't think you believed it."

"Don't you?"

"I don't know."

"If it wasn't an accident, you know, if he was pushed in, it would have had to be Nicola who did it?"

"Why?"

"Well, she'd a pretty stupendous motive, hadn't she? Sane or crazy, she thought he was trying to kill her. And no one else here had anything against Jocelyn."

"Hadn't they? Sitting here, I've been thinking. . . ."

"What about?"

"Alison."

She felt the arms around her slacken, then he withdrew one, though he kept the other round her shoulders.

"Why Alison? She's thousands of miles away."

"Yet she seems to keep cropping up."

"Isn't that natural? We're all very worried about her at the moment."

"Of course. And you're very fond of her, aren't you? Specially you, I mean. Yesterday you said something about there being a question of loyalty to someone. You couldn't tell me what you were thinking because of this loyalty. Wasn't it to Alison? Aren't you covering something up for her?"

His arm dropped from her shoulders. "Suppose you tell me in words of one syllable what you're getting at," he said.

"I'm not sure," Nina said. "I'm muddled. But I've been thinking of what Ruth said about seeing Jocelyn and Alison together on the path behind those bushes. I'd never thought of it before, because when you first told him about her being in London he hardly seemed to remember her. But now I'm wondering if there wasn't something between them."

"And?"

"Was there, Bill?"

He pressed his hands together, then let them fall apart, as if he were yielding something up.

"Yes, there was, though he was here for only a few days. But a week or two after he'd gone, Alison insisted on going on a visit to Sydney and Jocelyn was there too then, doing some broadcasts and so on. And it was after she came back that she started talking about going to an art school in London. Yes, I guess there was a good deal between them."

"And that's why you seemed so surprised at Heathrow when he asked so vaguely if Alison wasn't the pretty one."

"Did I seem surprised? Yes, that was why."

"And you think she followed Jocelyn to London, even though she knew he'd married, and you think, or perhaps you know, that they've been seeing each other. And that's the real reason why she never went near him and Nicola in their home. It had nothing to do with not intruding on their grief, or concealing the fact that she'd an illegitimate baby."

He gave a heavy sigh. "You seem to know it all."

"But that baby isn't Jocelyn's, Bill. You know that. It couldn't have been."

He did not answer.

"Is it Ern's?" she asked.

"He says not," he said, "and he's an honest sort of bloke. I don't know anyone else she was seeing much of at the time. But then with Alison you never knew. It could have been an odd pickup, someone she never saw again. There've been several of those. But I still love her, you know. It's a thing I can't help."

"If the baby was Ern's," Nina said, "wouldn't that give him a motive for killing Jocelyn?"

Again he did not answer. They had withdrawn a little from one another on the step.

She went on, "You see, if Ern didn't know he had a child until you came back after seeing Alison—"

"Oh, I understand what you mean all right," he said. "You're saying that finding Alison had left him for Jocelyn when she was actually going to have his child made Ern crazy with jealousy, and you're probably going to point out that he had the opportunity to kill Jocelyn too. On his own admission he went down to the river alone. Ruth followed him some minutes later. So if he'd happened to run into Jocelyn there, he could have pushed him into the river, gone in after him, and actually been holding him under the water when Ruth turned up and he shouted at her to go and get help. Yes, he could have done that."

"Only you don't think he did."

"You see, I know Ern. He isn't that sort of feller."

"Does anyone know anyone?"

"Perhaps not," he said. "All the same, I'm inclined to think you didn't kill Jocelyn yourself simply because I've got to know you a little. But I could be wrong. And you'd a motive too."

"I had?" She jerked her head round to look at him again.

"Yes, weren't you Jocelyn's girl before he came out to Australia the first time? We'd heard all about you from Brenda. So we were all surprised when we heard he'd married Nicola. I wonder what it was that man had. He had you all on a string. Intelligent girls too."

"Perhaps we were a little too intelligent. He seemed so subtle and quiet, yet gave you the feeling there was steel under the surface. But it's all ages ago, so far as I'm concerned.

He hasn't meant anything to me for a long time. If I'd ever wanted to murder him, it would have been when he married. I hated him then for a time. But I'd never have come on this journey with the two of them if I still did."

"But if it wasn't an accident, somebody hated somebody, didn't they? Somebody who probably knew Jocelyn well. Murder's generally an intimate sort of thing. It happens in a small world, a little shut-in world of violent feelings."

"So you're sure it was Nicola."

"If it wasn't an accident."

"It's true there doesn't seem to be any case against anyone else. You say it couldn't have been Ern, and I can't think of any reason why Ruth should have wanted to kill Jocelyn, or why your parents should either. Adrian and Brenda I suppose could have been after Jocelyn's money, but only if they could be sure Nicola would be convicted of his murder. You can't benefit financially by a crime you've committed, can you? But if Nicola couldn't inherit anything . . ." She paused as a thought struck her. "Bill, what do you do with murderers in Australia? Do you hang them?"

"Not in New South Wales. Officially they still do in Victoria and South Australia and Western Australia, but the sentences are never carried out. Don't start brooding about that now. What were you going to say about Nicola?"

"Just that if she can't inherit anything, Adrian and Brenda would get it all. Only how could they be certain she'd be found guilty?"

"And that leaves me," Bill said.

"Yes, but all I can think of against you is that you're hiding something," Nina said. "There's still something about your attitude to Alison that I don't understand. Is it something to do with what happened in Sydney? Did she and Jocelyn get married? Is his marriage to Nicola bigamous? Is it something like that? If it were, I suppose Alison is the one who'd inherit his money, isn't she?"

"Having arranged with me to split the proceeds if I got rid of him for her," Bill suggested. "There's your case for you, handed to you on a plate."

"Oh, Bill, you're laughing at me now."

"I've got to laugh, or take you by the throat and choke you."

As he spoke, taking her by surprise, he folded his hands around her throat.

At the first touch they were gentle, then they slid down her spine and he drew her close to him again and his mouth came down on hers. For a moment she was startled into a mood of perfect acceptance. It was to this, of course, that the whole argument had been leading up. Hadn't she known it, aimed at it all along?

A telephone started ringing.

Bill let her go, jumped to his feet, and shot into the house. Nina followed. She saw that Ruth had reached the telephone ahead of Bill. Ruth was a person who would always be first at the telephone, sure or hoping that the call would be for her. But after listening to the voice that spoke to her for only a moment, she gasped out, "Wait—please wait a moment! You want my father."

He was at her elbow by then and took the telephone from her.

"Ed Furness," she said. Her face had gone dead white.

"Yes, Ed?" Henry said. He listened, then said, "I see. . . . Yes. . . . Where was it? . . . Oh? When? . . . I see. Well, thanks for letting us know. . . . Yes, I'll tell them. . . . Yes, that would be best."

He put the telephone back on its rest.

"It's Nicola," he said. "They've found her. She drove the

car off the road into a tree. She was thrown forward through the windscreen, cut herself to pieces and got crushed against the steering wheel. She's dead."

"Dead!" It was Brenda, high and shrill.

No one else spoke.

Henry rubbed the back of his hand against his forehead. When he spoke again, his voice had lost its incisiveness. It was a tired, old man's voice.

"She was on the road to Melbourne, about two hundred and eighty miles from here. There was a witness of the accident. He said she'd been doing a steady eighty ahead of him when she suddenly started to wobble all over the road, then went off it and slapped into a tree. They think she'd probably gone to sleep. They're bringing her body here." He looked at Adrian. "Was that the thing to tell them to do?"

Adrian looked confused and helpless.

Brenda answered for him, "Yes, of course."

"Then she and Jocelyn can be buried together," Winnie said. "Oh, the poor girl. But after losing her husband and her child, perhaps it's a kind of mercy."

"At least she won't be tried for murder," Ruth said.

Her mother whirled on her. "Ruth, you are not to say things like that! I don't know what's come over you these last few days. Jocelyn's death was an accident, we all know that. And now I think we should all go up to bed. We're all very tired and there's nothing any of us can do any more and I'm sure Adrian and Brenda would like to be alone. It's been a terrible day for all of us, but worst of all for them. And for Nina. Nina, Nicola was a very old friend, wasn't she? I can't tell you how sorry I am for you all."

With firmness, though still with a flow of condolences, which made it easy for the others to stay silent, she sent everyone up to bed.

Nina slept hardly at all that night. Her imagination was out of control, swinging between tragedy and a guilty sense of joy. The conflict kept her in a state of almost frantic wakefulness. For there was no question about it, the most important thing for her personally that had happened that evening had been during the short time that she had spent with Bill, sitting on the steps of the verandah. But each time she started to relive the moments that had counted, her thoughts lurched away to show her images of dead faces, the one pale and drowned, the other cut to pieces by jagged glass and red with blood.

Several times she got up and wandered about the room, but she could escape neither those faces, each of which belonged to someone whose life had been interwoven with hers, if not always happily, for a long time, nor the exultation that flooded her when she thought of Bill. Was she some sort of monster, she wondered, to be able to think so much of herself when her friends were dead? It was already daylight before she fell asleep.

She then slept late. When she went downstairs she found a gloomy group of people in the dining room. Ern Wilding, of course, had gone home the evening before, and Henry was absent, but all the rest were there. They had had breakfast but did not seem to know what to do with themselves next. They were talking about how Adrian, Brenda, and Nina were to return to Adelaide, now that their car had been smashed up.

"Don't worry," Bill said, "I'll drive you."

"Oh, you can't do that, Bill," Brenda protested. "We'll fly from Mildura."

"No, I'll take you." He sounded intent on it, a little beyond the point of mere courtesy. "I've one or two things I can see to when I'm there." He turned to Nina, who was being helped to fried eggs and bacon by Winnie. "We've heard from Ed Furness about the autopsy, Nina. Jocelyn died by drowning, not from the blow on his head. That must have happened somehow when he fell and stunned himself and that was why he drowned. So it looks as if mother was right and it was an accident."

"And Nicola died by accident too," Ruth said, "so everything's nice and tidy."

"Ruth! Haven't I told you, you are not to say such things?" her mother cried. "It's not merely discourteous, it's very cruel. You should consider the feelings of Adrian and Brenda. If you have no feelings yourself, you might remember that other people have."

"Sorry," Ruth said without sounding in the least sorry. Yet her face was pallid, with patches of nervous colour on it. It occurred to Nina that the girl was forcing herself to seem hard-boiled because, in a simple and childish fashion, she was deeply scared by death. "I suppose I'd be upset if it was Bill who'd drowned. Or Alison. Would I, do you think? I've never lost anyone close to me. So I don't know what I'd feel, or for how long. But I've noticed with some people they actually seem a bit relieved when one of their relations dies, particularly if they're going to inherit some money from them."

"Shut up!" her brother said.

"Oh, I don't mean that's how Adrian and Brenda would feel," Ruth went on with a deliberate candour that was beginning to sound like slyness. "I was just making a general observation. Though I suppose Jocelyn had quite a lot of money to leave, and Adrian's his nearest relation. Or would it go to Nicola's nearest relation? She outlived him, didn't she? I suppose it would depend on what sort of wills they'd made—"

"Please!" Brenda sprang up from her chair, pressing her

handkerchief to her mouth. "I can't stand it! *Money!*" She spat the word out as if the taste of it made her feel sick.

Adrian touched her arm. "It's all right, she doesn't mean anything."

Ruth was looking dismayed at what she had done. "I'm sorry, Brenda," she said with a shake in her voice. "I'm a fool. I'm horrid. Don't take any notice of me."

"Anyway, Adrian isn't Jocelyn's nearest relation," Bill said. "His nearest relation is Brigid."

It was a remark that brought a complete silence.

He got up from the table and helped himself to more tea.

After a moment, sounding surprised, Adrian said, "Of course."

Brenda slowly sat down again.

"Brigid's dead," she said dully. "Jocelyn and Nicola knew that, or they'd never have come on this journey."

"There's no evidence she's dead," Bill said.

There was another silence, during which, for some reason, no one seemed to want to look at anyone else, except that Nina looked curiously at Bill, wondering what he had in mind.

"So now I suppose we get into some ghastly legal tangle," Brenda said in the same heavy tone as before. "Lawyers, letters—I expect Adrian will have to go to England—and all to no purpose. Of course, if there were the slightest chance of Brigid's being alive, if she could be found . . . But what's the good of hoping?"

"Hope's always a good thing," Winnie said. "Wonderful things can happen."

"And bloody awful things too," Ruth said. "Now, for God's sake, what are we going to do with ourselves? We can't spend the whole day sitting here?"

For once no one told her to keep quiet, and the gathering began to break up.

The rest of the day passed with dreary slowness. There seemed to be nothing to do but wait. Sergeant Furness returned and talked to Henry and Winnie and went away again. Bill and his father went off to the winery, although the day was another holiday and there was nothing much to occupy them there, but at least it filled the time for them. Winnie found some domestic things to do. Ruth roamed around restlessly, then suggested that she should take Nina, Brenda, and Adrian for a drive. Brenda declined for Adrian and herself, but Nina accepted the offer, and Ruth, saying that she imagined that Nina might like to see a sheep station, drove her off to visit the Wildings.

Nina brought back a confused impression of some friendly people, of acres of dusty scrub with some disconsolate-looking sheep nibbling away at it, of kangaroos, one of them a great red-brown monster, taller than a man, that appeared suddenly among the sparse trees and went leaping wildly away with enormous bounds, and of emus that did not flee from the car but came racing up to it, then stayed alongside it, running easily, until they suddenly lost interest in it and, crossing the road in front of it at peril of their lives, disappeared into the bush. Nina was given lunch by the Wildings and told the grazier's tale of woe, of how, from being among the richest men in the country, they were almost losing their livelihoods through the introduction of synthetic fabrics.

On the way back to Elderwood, Ruth said, "You know, Ern grew up thinking he was going to be rich, and now in fact he isn't. The Wildings are trying to go over to cattle, but their land isn't really suitable. The story's just the opposite of Jocelyn's, isn't it? He grew up fairly poor and then struck oil. It must have been a wonderful feeling. But I expect you think

I was poison, talking about money this morning. And forgetting about Brigid. It's a fact, I'd absolutely forgotten about her till Bill said what he did. I felt terrible when I realised that. I mean, just to have forgotten. But really, I'm not cold-blooded. It's just that—well, do you think there's the slightest chance she's alive?"

"There was a theory at the time she'd been taken by some unbalanced woman," Nina answered, "say, someone who'd lost a child of her own, or had a miscarriage, or an abortion that she discovered she hadn't really wanted, and if that's what happened, she may have looked after Brigid perfectly well. But that doesn't mean it'll be possible to find her after all this time. If this woman's got away with it for so long, there isn't any reason why she should be discovered now."

"But now that Brigid's an heiress—no," Ruth said, "I'm being stupid. I was going to say, now Brigid's an heiress the woman might want to come forward. But of course she can never do that without getting herself into bad trouble. So Brigid, if she's alive, may grow up quite poor, unless she somehow discovers her identity when she's older. D'you think that could happen?"

"Not unless the woman kept some proof of who she was, and if she's the kind of person we think she is, she probably destroyed everything that could possibly suggest Brigid isn't her own child."

"So she might as well be dead."

"Except from her own point of view. For all we know, she may have quite a good sort of life."

"Even with a mother who's mad enough to do what that woman did? My mother's about the sanest person I know. I can't think what it would be like to grow up with a mother whose sanity you didn't absolutely trust."

"Anyway, we'll never know."

"I don't suppose so."

They returned to Elderwood to find that during their absence the house had been invaded by the press. Jocelyn's death was news and reporters and photographers seemed to have sprung up out of the ground to get what they could in the way of a story. This was less than it might have been if the police had been ready to admit that they suspected foul play, but this they were refusing to do. They had settled for Winnie's commonsense theory that Jocelyn had been tripped up by one of his own shoelaces. There was no evidence to contradict it. That Nicola's death was an accident was never in doubt.

When Nina appeared with Ruth, the reporters surged round her, asking her questions about the Foleys' background, about the reason for their visit to Australia, about Brigid. Was it true that they had had their daughter kidnapped? The reporters were only quite amiable young men, doing their job in their normal way, but Nina suddenly hated them all with an intensity that made her feel that at any moment she might break into violent tears. Tears had been pent up in her all day. She trembled with anger and shock. Bill saw it, pushed his way past the most importunate of the questioners, grabbed Nina by the arm, and hustled her upstairs.

He followed her into her room. Its sombre Victorian sedateness made it feel a wonderful refuge from the pressures of the world outside.

"I'm sorry about that," he said.

"It doesn't matter. It took me by surprise, that's all." She dropped into a chair. "I'm very tired. I didn't sleep."

"Would you like a cup of tea, or a drink, or anything?"

"No, thank you."

"The inquest's tomorrow, and Adrian and my father have fixed up the funeral for the morning after, and then I'll drive you back to Adelaide." He was standing in front of her, his hands in his pockets. "And then I suppose you'll be flying back to England."

"I suppose so."

"Soon?"

"I haven't thought about it." She pushed a hand through her hair, which was moist with the heat of the afternoon and dusty from the drive around the sheep station. "But I think the sooner the better. For one thing, you know, Jocelyn was paying my expenses, but from now on I'll be on my own, so I'd better get back while my money lasts."

"Nina—" He walked away to a window and stood apparently gazing thoughtfully at the medallion of stained glass in the middle of it, which portrayed a Highland loch. "I want to go back with you."

It was a statement that might have been taken several ways. Nina decided, when she felt how her heart suddenly thudded, to wait for him to go on.

"I'd hoped there might be some way round it," he said, "but there isn't. I'll have to go."

So he was not thinking of flying round the world again for the pleasure of her company. She was glad that she had not answered him before.

"Why, if you don't want to?" she asked.

He tapped the panel of brightly coloured glass with a fingernail.

"If I tell you," he said, "will you promise me to let me handle things in my own way?"

"How can I stop you, whatever you mean?"

"You could quite easily."

"How?"

"By going to the police and telling them what I want to tell you. It would be quite simple."

She looked at his sturdy outline against the window and wished that she could see his face.

"I think I trust you enough to promise," she said. "Go on."

"It's all right, I shan't hold you to the promise, if you don't want to keep it. I know it's a thing I shouldn't have asked you."

"I'll probably keep it all the same. Only I wish I knew what we're talking about."

"About Alison, of course. It's always Alison, isn't it? As you said, she keeps cropping up. But I hoped somehow I could keep her out of things. She doesn't deserve it. She's gone nearly as low as a person can. But I keep hoping I can straighten things out without her being made to suffer too much. I want her to have another chance. If Nicola had lived, I think I could have managed it, but now I simply don't know what to do. With Jocelyn dead, I don't think it'll be difficult to get Alison to admit the truth, at least to me, though all I've got at present are certain suspicions. There's an odd set of facts that fit together in a peculiar way. . . ." He turned, leaning against the window sill, to look at Nina. "I'm talking about Brigid, of course."

She jerked forward in her chair, then came to her feet.

"Bill, you aren't saying Alison is the woman who stole her!"

"Oh no," he said, "Jocelyn did that. And he gave her to Alison to keep until he could get rid of Nicola. He loved that child of his desperately. And he loved Alison too, and he wanted to have them both. But even if Nicola would have divorced him for Alison, she'd never have let him keep Brigid. So for him to be able to keep Brigid, Nicola had to be killed. Those attempts of his to kill her, Nina, they were real. I told you I thought there was a rational motive behind them, didn't I? Well, if going after what you want without caring about anyone else is rational, what could have been more cold-bloodedly rational than Jocelyn's motive?"

Chapter Twelve

From the way that they looked at one another, they might have been in the midst of a quarrel. Then Nina backed away to her chair and sat down.

"You can't believe that," she said. "If you did, you'd have done something about it."

"What?" he asked.

"I don't know. Warned Nicola. Warned me. Something."

"On suspicion?"

"Is it really only on suspicion?"

"I told you, some facts fit together in a peculiar way, that's all."

"And in any case, you'd try to protect Alison. That loyalty of yours. She comes first with you."

"Not really. Shall I tell you about it?"

"Yes."

He turned to the window again, as if he did not want to look at her while he spoke, but then he turned back and it occurred to Nina that something in his face had changed. The guardedness that had been there from the start had gone. That apparently open and direct look that in fact revealed so little about him was really open and direct now. He had abandoned his defences.

"When I went over to London a few weeks ago," he said,

"it was partly on business, as I told Jocelyn, but mostly it was because we were worried about Alison. We hadn't had a letter from her for six months. And it wasn't just that she was a person who didn't write letters. She'd written to us often before that. But all of a sudden she stopped. So I was supposed to visit her and find out if all was well. I went to the address she'd given us—it was a boardinghouse of sorts—and they told me there she'd moved out six months before and hadn't left a forwarding address. They'd been sending any letters that came for her on to the art school. So I went to the place and found that the only address they had was the one I'd just come from. And they were a bit worried about her, because her attendance had dropped off badly recently. But I managed to get in touch with one of her teachers, and he told me the names of one or two students she'd seemed to be friendly with and I picked one of them up and she knew where Alison was living, although she was very cagey about giving me the address. I knew, after I'd talked to that girl, that something was wrong, though all I really suspected was that I'd find Alison living with some man."

As he talked, he had begun to move about the room.

"When I went to the address I'd been given," he went on, "Alison was expecting me. The girl I'd talked to had phoned her, saying she'd given me the address. And Alison wasn't at all glad to see me. She asked why couldn't we leave her alone and acted as if she didn't mean to let me in. But she knew she couldn't really keep me out, and when I went in, there was the baby. A very nice baby, as babies go, I suppose, and obviously well looked after, though the flat was a mess, the kind I'd expect Alison to live in. It's a mews flat in Chelsea and villainously expensive, I should think, and full of artist's clutter. Alison was violently on the defensive at first, while I did my best to take it all as a matter of course, because there wasn't much point in doing anything else. I asked her how old the baby was and she said six months and that she'd been pregnant when she left home and that was why she'd wanted to get away. I asked her who the father was, but she wouldn't tell me. I asked her if they were going to marry and she said no. I asked her what her plans for the future were and she told me to mind my own business. So far, in its way, it was all quite normal. I rather thought, from signs about the place, that a man was living there with her, but he couldn't be the father of the child if she'd been pregnant before she left Australia, unless he'd come over with her. Anyway, I didn't ask her about him. I only told her that if she'd had the sense to go on writing home, I shouldn't have come hunting for her, and she could have kept her secret. Then all of a sudden she burst into tears and clung to me and told me she wished she'd never left home, because then none of it would have happened. That didn't make sense to me if it was true she'd got pregnant here. And it had to be true, because of the age of the child. Then I began to think about its age. . . ."

He had returned to the window and was standing with his back to it, gripping the sill with both hands.

"I know next to nothing about kids," he said, "but it struck me that that one was pretty precocious for six months. She was crawling around on the floor in a very independent way and she was big too. But none of us had noticed any signs of pregnancy when Alison left home, so the baby couldn't possibly be much more than that. I thought to myself, it's the vitamins and things they give them nowadays and they must grow up faster than they used to, and I didn't think much more about it for the moment. Alison got over her crying fit and for a while we were quite friendly. Then I asked her if she'd thought of having the baby adopted, and for some reason she began to laugh in a hysterical way and told me I didn't know how funny I was being. I thought at the time she meant I was a fool not to understand her maternal feelings better, but now I believe she was laughing at me because I'd got the whole thing upside down, because Jocelyn had made her do the adopting. Well, I stayed for a while and then it was time for the baby to have her bath and Alison took her off to her bedroom to undress her, and I was following, talking, when suddenly Alison slammed the door in my face and yelled at me to go away and not keep spying on her. But she was just too late, because I'd seen past her into the room and there was Jocelyn's photograph on the dressing table." One of Bill's hands balled into a fist and pounded the window sill. "And that child's the image of Jocelyn. I hadn't thought of it till I saw the photograph, though something about her had been worrying me, but that's what it was, the likeness."

"Brigid was very like Jocelyn," Nina said. "Even when she was a few weeks old, you could see it. But she'd got Nicola's colouring, dark hair and dark eyes."

"Alison's child has dark hair and dark eyes," Bill said. "And Alison's hair is red gold and her eyes are blue, and there wasn't a trace of her features in the child's face. But even then, when I saw the photograph of Jocelyn and noticed the resemblance, I didn't start to understand the situation. Of course, I knew the Foleys had lost their child, but I didn't dream for a moment that Alison could be involved in any way."

"When did you think of it?" Nina asked.

"I'll come to that. Looking back, it seems to me I was very slow about it. But it's quite a thing to think of, you know, that your sister may be involved in a thing like kidnapping. It isn't just the first thing you think of when you see her. When I saw that photograph of Jocelyn what I thought was that the old affair had started up again. And that was worrying enough. It seemed to me Alison was set on making as much of a disaster of her life as she was able. But I didn't see far beyond that till Jocelyn tried to push Nicola under that lorry in Mexico City. And even then I couldn't really believe what I'd started to think."

"Did you follow him to Mexico on purpose?"

"Yes. That evening in London, when the baby had been put to bed, Alison and I had a long talk. She'd been doing some thinking while she was busy with the baby and she'd got her story ready. She was in love with Jocelyn, she said, and always had been and always would be and so on, but I was quite wrong if I thought she was having an affair with him. She'd hardly seen him since she'd got to London. They'd met once or twice, she said, but he'd made it quite plain he was sticking to his wife, and specially since they'd lost their child, he'd got to, or she'd go mad, and in a few days' time he was taking her off round the world to see if that would help her. It was quite a good story except for one thing. Alison knew too much about the Foleys' plans, when they were leaving, where they were stopping and so on. So it was obvious she'd seen Jocelyn recently. And I'm generally able to guess when she's lying. She does a good deal of it, yet she's never been really clever at it. She gets too innocent, too candid, she adds too many artistic touches that don't quite fit. I was sure by the time I left her that the affair with Jocelyn was on. And suddenly I asked myself if the baby could possibly be his. Had he been out here sometime last year without any of us knowing about it? And then I thought, why shouldn't I go home by the same route as Jocelyn, pick up with him and see for myself what the situation seemed to be? And you know what happened when I went up to him. He pretended he didn't even remember Alison clearly. 'Was she the pretty one?' he asked. He couldn't have thought I'd be fooled, because he'd have heard from Alison that I'd been to see her, but he wanted to fool Nicola for the time being and hoped I'd play along. Well, I didn't want to interfere at that point. No one's ever been able to stop Alison doing what she wanted and her life was her own, as I saw it, and I very nearly didn't join up with the Foleys in Mexico at all. Only it happened that you were along with the Foleys, weren't you? And that made me want to stick around. And then that accident happened in front of the cathedral."

"But you didn't do anything."

"Nina, what could I do? Will you ask yourself that? What *could* I do? I saw Jocelyn fall against Nicola and it could easily have been a real accident. But for the first time I thought it could be that he wanted to get rid of her and marry Alison. But why shouldn't there simply be a divorce, if there wasn't something more to it than I'd understood so far? And then I thought of that child and how precocious she was, and how she looked so like Jocelyn and had Nicola's colouring, and how a divorce wouldn't help Jocelyn if the child was really Brigid and what he wanted was to have both her and Alison for himself. He'd have to get rid of Nicola, if that was the way things were. That was the only thing for him to do. But tell me, is that the sort of thing that it's easy to believe in? It isn't easy to believe your sister's involved in a peculiarly horrible sort of criminal conspiracy. The mere fact that she'd have to be, if you were right, would tend to make you think you were just giving yourself nightmares. And I'd no solid evidence. If I'd challenged Jocelyn, he'd have laughed at me. If I'd spoken to Nicola and been wrong, I'd only have made her condition worse. I was helpless. So I came home. What else was there to do?"

"And you did try to warn me, didn't you?" Nina said. "Only I didn't pay much attention."

"Perhaps I didn't say as much as I might have," Bill replied.

"What makes you so sure now your guess about Brigid is right?" she asked.

"What you've told me about Jocelyn's other attempts on Nicola's life."

"But you still want to protect Alison, even though you believe now she's involved in this criminal conspiracy."

He lifted his hands, holding them out to Nina for an instant, then let them fall. There was painful supplication in the gesture.

Aware that she was setting a pattern for the future, showing that she would nearly always be ready to do anything he asked her, she said, "How can it be done?"

He answered quickly, "It's just a case of getting her to return the baby, isn't it? I expect she's got some means of identification, like the clothes Brigid wore when she was taken, or perhaps some toy she had. And there could be a note pinned to her clothes saying, 'This is the Foley baby.' Then Alison could tell her friends she'd had the baby adopted. It's the sort of thing a crowd like that wouldn't bother to inquire into too deeply. And she might disappear from the scene for a time, go to Paris or somewhere. I don't think it would be difficult to persuade her to do it, now that Jocelyn's dead. I doubt if she ever wanted Brigid for herself. It was only because Jocelyn wanted her so badly that Alison took her on."

"But whom does she return Brigid to, now that Jocelyn and Nicola are dead?" Nina asked.

"I was thinking of you," he said. "That's why I wanted to talk about all this."

"The traditional place is the steps of a church."

"But she might not be found at once, and January in London is a chilly place. And the steps of a police station would be rather risky. Alison could so easily be seen leaving her there. So that suggests your doorstep. She'd be safe with you."

"And then?" Nina said. "What do I do with Brigid when I find her?"

"Get in touch with the police immediately. But remember to forget every single thing I've been saying to you."

"And then?"

"Then I should think Adrian and Brenda would adopt her. They've no children of their own and they could give her a good sort of life."

She nodded thoughtfully. "Yes, it could work. I suppose it's the best thing to do. It won't help Brigid if Alison's share in it is all dragged out into the light, and it would be hell for your parents and Ruth and you. All right then, on my doorstep, and the sooner the better."

A smile lit up his face.

"Yes, just as soon as they let us go," he said. "As soon as the inquest's over."

She realised that he anticipated no problems arising at the inquest.

He was right in this, for the verdicts on the deaths of both Jocelyn and Nicola were that they were accidental. If anyone had any doubts of the correctness of the verdicts, nothing was said about it. There was not much point in having Nicola posthumously convicted of having pushed Jocelyn into the river, and if anyone had done it, who could it have been but she? Who else could have known on that afternoon when everyone else was sleeping that he had gone down to the riverbank? Who else had such a strong motive? But she could not defend herself, and in any case, the evidence against

158

her was far from strong. A flapping shoelace was as likely to have been to blame as she was.

After the funeral came the long drive back to Adelaide.

By the time that they left Elderwood, Bill and Nina had worked out how they were going to arrange the journey back to London. It was a little complicated, because Bill did not want to have to explain to anyone why he had taken it into his head to return so soon after his last visit. So Nina, they had agreed, would make her arrangements to leave alone, then Bill would have an ungovernable impulse to follow her. To her it sounded an extremely expensive kind of ungovernable impulse to have, but that aspect of it did not seem to disturb Bill. They decided to break the journey in Singapore, then fly straight through to London.

Back in Glenelg, Brenda and Adrian made a not very insistent attempt to persuade Nina to stay on with them for a time.

"After all, it might save you an unnecessary journey," Brenda remarked as they sat over sandwiches and coffee after the drive from Elderwood. Bill, who had refused the offer of a room, had left them to go to an hotel in the city. "We're likely to see you back sometime soon, it seems to me. I'm delighted about it, of course. I'd simply love to have you living here. But I wonder if you could really stand Elderwood. Because you'll never get Bill to leave the old home, you know. You may as well face that fact about him before you get any deeper in than you are at present."

"I don't know actually how deep in we are," Nina said. "You're looking a bit far ahead. I'll go into Adelaide tomorrow and book my flight."

"Just as you like, but I can tell you how deep in you are quite easily," Brenda said. "You're crazy about one another. But remember, if you want him, you'll have to give up a lot of things. Your acting, for one."

"I'd be no great loss to the theatre," Nina said. "I've been thinking more and more of getting out of it anyway."

"Into what, for instance?"

"Oh, I don't know. Just a job of some sort."

"You won't have to worry about that if you marry Bill."

"We haven't been talking about marrying," Nina said irritably.

"Sorry," Brenda said. "You know how I always put my foot in things. I blurt out what comes into my head. I wish I were more like you, good at keeping my own counsel."

Nina gave her a quick look, wondering if somehow Brenda had guessed how many things she was keeping her own counsel about. Could she by chance have overheard any of the long talk that Bill and Nina had had about Alison and Brigid? But Brenda was chewing a chicken sandwich and her shrewd, sharp little face looked merely tired and not in the least as if she were probing for anything that Nina might be trying to hide.

She left for Singapore two days later.

Adrian and Brenda saw her off at the airport. Nina kissed them both, walked out to the plane, turned at the bottom of the steps, waved to them, then climbed on board. A steward showed her to her seat. She stowed her overnight case under it, fastened her seat belt, and for a moment, with nothing else to do but sit and wait for Bill to appear, felt a blind thankfulness to be on her way home, extricated from her involvement with Jocelyn and Nicola. But then she remembered abruptly what was still ahead of her and that she had not yet been extricated from her involvement with the dead, and as suddenly as that thankfulness had come, it changed into acute panic.

Suppose Bill did not follow her. Suppose he had had second thoughts about Alison and her baby. Suppose he had decided that the child was not Brigid at all, or that, even if she was, he was going to leave Alison to do whatever she wished with her. Suppose that after filling Nina's mind with horrible suspicions, but no certainties, he had gone home, leaving her alone to decide what she ought to do when she arrived in England. Suppose he was not in love with her. . . .

She discovered that she was feeling sick and dizzy with the conviction that he would not appear, that he had never cared for her any more than Jocelyn had, and that she would have to suffer all over again the misery of growing out of her own love. Then she saw Bill hurrying towards the plane and her head cleared. She felt a lot happier at the thought of the journey ahead of her than she felt she had any right to.

They had to change planes in Perth. In the plane in which they went on, an Indian stewardess in a pretty sari brought them glasses of champagne and cold towels with which to mop their steaming faces. Nina read a detective story that she had bought in the airport at Perth. Its scene was London and as she read on, dozed for a time, read a little more, then dozed again, London seemed to be reaching out to her, working its way into her thoughts, reminding her of winter, of cold, of grey, sodden clouds hanging low over the rooftops, and making her feel that the blue skies and warm seas of the last few weeks had been an improbable dream. A dream shot through with nightmare, from which she would be glad to wake, but also with a glittering charm to it. Already it seemed to have happened a long time ago, to have been left a long way behind. London had again become the reality of her life.

It was dark when the plane came down in Singapore. The air had a damp, stifling heat. The hotel in which the airline in Adelaide had booked rooms for her and Bill was a small one, staffed entirely by Chinese. The clerk at the reception desk was a smiling, slant-eyed young girl, dressed in the briefest of miniskirts, which her Chinese proportions turned into something almost as elegant as a *cheong sam*. There was a heavy aroma of curry and spices in the air to remind travellers that they were in Asia, but otherwise once the doors of their rooms were closed, they might have been in any hotel in any country in the world. The modern hotel has utterly overcome nationalism.

Tired enough to feel confused, Nina thought that by the morning she might have forgotten where she was. She went straight to bed, unpacking only her overnight bag. She could open her suitcase in the morning to get out the warmer clothes that she would need for the rest of the journey to London.

She woke in a room striped with bright sunshine through the slats of the venetian blinds. She got up, had a shower, dressed, opened her case and started to rummage in it.

There was a knock at the door.

"It's me," Bill said. "Can I come in?"

She opened the door to him.

He took a step into the room, then stood still. A very strange expression appeared on his face. He was staring down at the ground at Nina's feet.

Puzzled, she looked down too.

Coiled there like a pale brown snake on the carpet, was a shoelace. It had fallen, apparently, from the pocket of the scarlet beach wrap which she had just taken out of her suitcase and which she had not worn since she had gone down to swim in the river at Elderwood.

Chapter Thirteen

Nina and Bill travelled on to London that evening. They had talked about the shoelace and had agreed on its significance, then they had done their best to put the thought of it behind them for the present. They had spent part of the day doing a bus tour of the city, seeing the usual tall modern buildings that have mushroomed all over the earth, and China Town, distinguished mostly by its gay bunting of bright-coloured washing fluttering from every window, and the memorial to the civilian dead of the war, locally nicknamed the "four chopsticks." It consisted of four slender white columns, one symbolizing the Chinese dead, one the Malays, one the Indians, and one a group evasively referred to by the guide as Other Races.

They wandered through the mad fantasy of the Tiger Balm Gardens, a kind of zoo in which all the animals were made of plaster, much more than life-size, and painted in colours of appalling brilliance. High on a rock near the gateway, an enormous tiger, luridly striped and grinning fiercely, crouched as if ready to spring down upon the placid crowd that sauntered along the pathway below. To judge by the size of the crowd, the place was very popular.

The bus took its passengers on to something described as an Arts Centre, where the main attraction was a snake charmer who draped his snakes around the neck of anyone who wanted to be photographed wearing a necklace of writhing serpents. They writhed so languidly, however, were so lethargic, that it seemed probable that they had been heavily doped. In any case, the guide promised, they never bit tourists.

The day was swelteringly hot and humid. Thinking of the journey ahead, Nina lay down for the afternoon, then met Bill for dinner in the restaurant of the hotel where they ate Chinese food of a subtlety and richness unlike any that Nina had ever encountered in the proliferating Chinese restaurants of London. Then they set off for the airport.

The journey took eighteen hours. Breakfast was brought round at what felt like two in the morning, and another meal after the plane had touched down at Bahrein. Nina could not make up her mind whether this was lunch or dinner, but to face roast veal at that hour, whatever it was, felt sickening. She did not even attempt to eat it. Time went by in a daze of fatigue in which she was aware of very little but bodily discomfort and the deadly slowness with which the hours passed. She and Bill did not discuss what lay ahead of them. When they spoke to one another, it was with a reserved sort of consideration for one another's comfort and about very little else. Nina could not be sure whether this was because they had begun to feel that they knew each other so well and had no need to talk, or because, as they approached London, they were turning into strangers.

Heathrow meant greyness, cold, an overcoat, a headscarf, gloves.

A bitter wind was blowing and dark clouds went scurrying across a lowering sky. There was a bite in the January air that promised snow. Faces looked pinched and unnaturally white after the tanned skins of Australia. Bill and Nina took a taxi into London. Nina had a plan that Bill should spend the night in the Battersea flat, which she shared at present with a girl who worked in a publisher's office and another who was working for a Ph.D. in physics at a London college. This girl, Nina knew, had planned to spend Christmas with her family in Hull and would not have returned to the flat yet. But when Nina suggested to Bill that he could use the empty room, he shook his head.

"Won't do," he said. "If we arrange that Brigid's to be left on your doorstep, it's going to lead to the police descending on you, and the press too, and if I'm around there'd be awkward questions asked that could lead straight back to Alison. If you really mean to help me keep her out of trouble, I've got to keep out of sight as much as I can myself. You understand that, don't you?"

"Yes," she said reluctantly.

"You do want to do it still, don't you?" he asked. "If you're not sure, tell me now and give me a chance to think."

"I do," she said quickly to take the look of anxiety from his face. "But don't we meet again? Are you just going to vanish?"

"That isn't likely, is it?"

"I don't know. I don't seem able to think ahead. I'm too tired. When do we go to see Alison?"

"When you've had some sleep."

"You don't think it'd be better to get it over straightaway?"

"I don't think some sleep would do either of us any harm."

"All right." She leant her head against his shoulder. "But I don't really understand why you want me to see her at all. I'd have thought you could fix up everything without my being there. It might even be better that way."

"Except that you may be able to identify Brigid."

"After all this time? Babies change so."

"I'd still like you to be there to hear what Alison has to say. You may tell me I'm a fool from start to finish, that I've had the whole thing wrong all along."

"Which you half-hope is what I'll do."

"Of course, except that if the child is Brigid, if we've found her, that'll be worth while, won't it?"

"Yes. . . . You know, Bill, there's a thought I kept having from time to time on this flight. D'you think Nicola's death was really an accident?"

"Oh, you've been wondering about that, have you?"

She glanced up at his face. "You have too."

"Yes, but we'll never know."

"No. But it was Jocelyn who suggested to Nicola that she shouldn't come in swimming with us. And he left her passport and ticket where she could easily find them. And if he'd somehow put it into her head that it would be easy for her to take Brenda's keys and the car, and if he'd loosened a couple of bolts on the steering column, or something like that . . . You see, it wouldn't have mattered if it hadn't worked, but would have been so convenient if it had. And we'll never know if it did, as you said."

"And it doesn't much matter now."

"No. . . ." She felt sleep pressing on her in a dark cloud and was glad, after all, that he did not want to deal with Alison that day.

The taxi left her at her flat, then took Bill on to look for an hotel.

Half an hour later he telephoned to tell her where he was and to make sure that their arrangements for next day were clear in her mind. She was boiling eggs at the time, intending to go to bed as soon as she had eaten them, although it was still daylight. Neither of her friends was in the flat. She wrote a note to say that she was home, left it on the table in the passage, went to bed and did not wake until ten o'clock next morning.

She woke wondering at the brightness of the light in the room, then discovered that it had snowed in the night. The snow in the street had already been churned to a brownish slush, but it still lay clean and glistening on rooftops and window ledges and on the black branches of the trees along the edges of the pavements. The room felt icy cold. She lit the gas fire, put on a warm quilted dressing gown and fur-lined slippers, and had cornflakes and coffee sitting as close to the fire as she could. There was no one in the flat, but she had found a note addressed to her on the table where she had left her note the evening before. This one said, "Didn't want to wake you. Hope cutting things short didn't mean you had trouble. See you this evening—hear all your news then. Pam." Pam was the girl who worked for a publisher. She would have left the flat to catch her bus before Nina was awake.

Her room took a long time to warm up. But although she shivered, she could not quite convince herself that if only she shut her eyes and opened them again suddenly enough, she would not find that the sun was shining and the air was warm and fragrant. Presently she dressed in her warmest tweed suit, knee-high boots, and her sheepskin jacket and went out to meet Bill.

They had lunch in a small Greek restaurant not far from the mews where Alison lived.

Bill was so subdued that he seemed almost hostile, but Nina had begun to understand that when he seemed hostile it was because he had things on his mind that he could hardly bear to face.

"Nina, now that we're here, I'm dead scared," he said. "It all sounded easy when I first suggested it, this making Alison turn the baby over to you. But now it doesn't look as simple as it did on the other side of the world. Suppose she won't do it. Or suppose I'm getting you into something that leads to serious trouble for you. It's making you an accessory to a crime. I didn't think as much about all that as I should have."

"Let's not talk about it," Nina said, "or I'll start getting scared too. Let's just do what we decided. We both know all the problems."

"I wonder if we do," he said.

"Well, we can talk about it later, if we've got to."

They finished their lunch quickly, then walked to Alison's flat.

The mews was one of those that have been smartened up with plenty of bright paint and are very expensive. Bill rang the bell beside a pale blue door. A face appeared for a moment at a window above, then disappeared. Footsteps sounded on the stairs inside, the door opened and a girl looked out.

"Oh, it's you," she said to Bill in an irritated tone, as if it meant nothing to her that he had come halfway round the world to see her. "Who's she?"

"A friend of Nicola's—Nina Hemslow." To Nina he added, "My sister, Alison."

The girl stood still in the doorway. She did not ask them in. Suddenly Nina thought of Jocelyn asking Bill if Alison were not the pretty one of the family and of Bill's surprise at this. Later Bill had said that this had been because of what he had known of Jocelyn's relations with Alison. But that had not been the only reason. No one would dream of calling this girl pretty. If she was not actually ugly, then she was a beauty. There was the element of exaggeration about her that is usually necessary to beauty, a touch almost of the grotesque, that catches the eye at once, holds it with astonishment, and impresses itself unforgettably. She was tall, lean, angular. Her shoulders were wide, her hips were narrow, her breasts very small. Yet there was an intense, hungry femininity about her, both in her poise, her taut stillness as she stood there in the doorway, and in her narrow face with its high cheekbones, pale, hollow cheeks, blue eyes, and sullen mouth. It was an ardent, excitable face, ravaged already, although she was only in her early twenties, by explosive emotions very close to the surface. There was no innocence in her youth, but rather a formidable knowledge. Her hair was red gold, thick and straight, parted in the middle and hanging loosely round her shoulders. She was wearing a purple dress down to her ankles, a heavy silver cross hanging on a thick chain round her neck, and wooden-soled sandals.

She gave Nina only the briefest of glances and seemed to dismiss her.

"I told you not to come back," she said to Bill.

"Do I always do what I'm told?" he asked.

"It might sometimes be better if you did."

"Have you heard the news about Jocelyn, Alison?"

"Yes, it was on television."

"That must have been a shock for you, if that's how you heard it."

"It was."

"And you know about Nicola too?"

"Yes."

They gazed at one another in silence. The girl's face was a mask that looked as if it might crumple shockingly at any moment, Bill's had a wary affection in it.

After a pause, he said, "Hadn't you better let us in?"

"Why her?" Alison jerked her head towards Nina without looking at her. "I don't feel like meeting strangers at the moment."

"You'd better, all the same. She's going to help us."

"I don't need help."

From upstairs came the cry of a child. It was a cry of exasperation, demanding attention.

"Don't you?" Bill said.

"Go away!" she cried. "Go away! Just go away!"

"But everything's different now that Jocelyn's dead, isn't it?"

"D'you think I don't know that?" Tears swam suddenly in the brilliant blue eyes. "Oh, all right, come in. But don't try to interfere. I know what I have to do."

She turned and ran up the narrow flight of stairs behind her, her wooden soles clattering on the steps. Bill and Nina followed her.

She took them into a room that overlooked the mews. It was long and narrow and had probably once been two rooms, at some time turned into one. The flat had plainly been expensively converted from the coachman's little house that it had originally been and now had central heating, fine woodblock floors, and ostentatious wallpapers.

It was in overwhelming disorder. There were paints and brushes on the chairs and tables, a curious collection of stones, pieces of rope, coils of wire, knives, scissors, rolls of paper scattered about everywhere, and canvases stacked around the walls. No finished work was on view. Nina wondered if Alison was one of the people who never quite finish anything. Mixed up with all the rest of the muddle were a child's garments, and the child herself, still shrieking with annoyance at being disregarded, was on the floor in the middle of the room.

She was a rosy-cheeked child with curly black hair and dark eyes, and she was wearing a yellow knitted dress which had some smears of green paint on it. She had some of the same green paint on her plump, pink hands and in her hair. She seemed to Nina much too big to be six months old.

"Oh God, I'll have to clean her up," Alison said, picking the baby up and starting to jog her up and down in a rather perfunctory manner. "If I take my eyes off her for a minute she's poking into everything. If I'd known how much trouble she was going to be, I don't think I'd ever have taken her on. At first I thought it was going to be fun, but in fact I've given up almost everything else, just to look after her. But you can't say I haven't done it properly. She's a healthy creature. I've done what I said I would."

"Fun?" Bill said. "It was fun to steal another woman's child and send her half out of her mind? This child *is* Brigid Foley, isn't she?"

"Of course she is," Alison answered indifferently. "I thought you worked that out last time you were here."

"I just wanted to hear you say it," he said.

"Well, I've said it. And now why don't you go?"

"Can you prove who she is?"

"Prove it?" Her voice shot up unsteadily. "You've only to look at her. She's so like Jocelyn, I can hardly bear to look at her now. D'you know what it's done to me, hearing of his death? Talk of driving that woman Nicola out of her mind, what d'you think's happened to me? Hearing about his death like that—fatal accident to famous writer and a photograph of him, and then on to some bloody news about football— what d'you think that was like, all alone here, with no one I could turn to?"

"Don't try to play too hard on my sympathy," Bill said, "or you may use up the little I've got. Have you any proof of the child's identity, the kind that would convince the police?"

"Oh, the police," she said. "That's your idea of helping me, to turn me in to the police."

"It's what I ought to do," he said. "You've done an unspeakably horrible thing."

"What's so horrible about it?" she demanded. "That woman Nicola was no good. She never really cared for Jocelyn and he never cared for her. She tricked him into marrying her, wanting his money and the prestige of being the wife of someone like him. He told me all about it. He only stuck it as long as he did for Brigid's sake. He told me what a hell of a life he had with Nicola, how unstable she was and what a mess she was making of bringing up Brigid."

"Are you an outstanding example of stability yourself?" Bill asked.

"If I'm not, I've got other things he needed," she answered.

"I'm sure you have. But you seem to have got hold of a rather one-sided view of Jocelyn's life story."

"If it's one-sided to love him, to love him with all my heart, to accept him as he was, all right, I have," she said. "Have you ever loved anyone with all your heart, Bill? In case you haven't, let me warn you, it does make you one-sided. And that's wonderful. You haven't any doubts about whose side you're on and what you ought to do."

"What a pity then that all that feeling got wasted on a man like Jocelyn Foley," Bill said, his voice growing calmer as the girl's excitement rose. "You haven't answered my question yet, have you any positive proof of the child's identity?"

She shrugged her shoulders. "I've got the clothes she was wearing when Jocelyn handed her over to me. I've got a pink teddy bear she was clutching. She's chewed it half to pieces, but I suppose someone might recognise it."

"I might," Nina said. "I gave it to her."

"But what does it matter?" Alison said. "I told you I know what I've got to do. I'm stuck with her and I'll go on looking after her. I'll never harm her. You needn't be afraid. I'm not a monster."

"You're not?" Bill said. "That's funny, it's what I'd more or less made up my mind you were. A monster you couldn't help being. But it won't do, Alison. She's got to be given back where she belongs."

"Just tell me where she belongs, poor little devil!" Alison said. "Her mother and father are both dead. Who's she got but me?"

"She's got relations. And she happens to have a lot of money, which she's entitled to inherit."

"So I'm to hand her to the police and go to gaol myself for kidnapping, all for the sake of her money. What a nice brother you are. Only I'll tell you something, it probably wasn't kidnapping at all. All I did was look after her when her own father brought her to me. Is that a crime?"

"In the circumstances, I should think it was," Bill said. "With the police hunt on for her, and the newspapers and television showing her photograph and Jocelyn himself offering a reward for information leading to her being found, I should think at least it was criminal conspiracy. But listen, Alison, I'm not going to ask you to turn her in to the police. I realise that could be dangerous for you, and for the sake of them all at home I'm hoping we can cover up what you've done. But you've got to do what I tell you. You're going to put Brigid in a pram, or a cot, or something, with those clothes of hers and the pink teddy bear, and you're going to write a note saying 'This is Brigid Foley,' which you'll pin to her dress, and you're going to leave her outside Nina's door tonight, ring the bell and run for it. And Nina will be waiting with a friend she shares the flat with who'll be a witness to just how it happened, and Nina will give you a little time to get clear, then get in touch with the police and you can fade out—"

The doorbell rang.

Alison took no notice of it. She went on jogging Brigid up and down. Brigid by now had deposited a bright green streak on Alison's cheek. It made her look as if she had been experimenting with some barbaric kind of make-up.

"It wouldn't work," she said. "The first thing she'd do is tell the police about me." As before, she spoke as if Nina were not there.

"I don't think she will," Bill said. "We're rather one-sided about each other, she and I. What she promises me, she'll do."

"Oh." Alison glanced at Nina at last. "Is that how it is?"

The bell rang again.

Alison went to the window and looked down. "Some damned woman," she said. "Probably collecting for something. I'd better get rid of her."

She dumped Brigid on the floor and went running down the stairs with a noisy clattering of her wooden-soled sandals.

Nina heard her open the door and start to say something. Then suddenly she shouted out, "What the hell d'you think you're doing?" There was a thudding sound, as if a blow had been struck, then quick, light footsteps came up the stairs and Brenda burst panting into the room.

She looked at Brigid on the floor, at Bill and Nina, and exclaimed, "So I was right, you *were* plotting something! Thank God I got here in time to stop it!"

Alison appeared in the doorway behind Brenda.

"She's mad," Alison said. "You'd better cope with her, Bill."

He said, "You didn't waste much time getting here, Brenda."

"I've come straight from the airport," she said. She looked as if she had. Her brownish-yellow eyes were red-rimmed with fatigue, her face was waxy white between her freckles. She was wearing a grey trouser suit and a grey tweed overcoat and had a woollen headscarf knotted under her chin. She turned to Nina. "It looks lucky I did too. I'd never have thought you'd lend yourself to anything like this, Nina."

"How did you know where to come?" Bill asked.

"I got Alison's new address from your mother," Brenda said. "I thought I'd better after I'd listened to you and Nina talking up in Nina's room about Alison having Brigid." She looked round the room. "I want the telephone. I want the police here and I want Brigid identified and I want to take her home with me."

"And you want her money too, I expect," Bill said. "I wonder just how long she'd last in your loving care. I believe even Alison would do better for her." He put a hand in his pocket, drew out a pale brown shoelace and dangled it in front of Brenda. "Take a look at this before you do anything you might regret."

She looked blankly at the shoelace.

"I don't understand," she said.

"Don't you remember Jocelyn's missing shoelace?" he said. "When we got him out of the river one of his shoelaces was undone, the other was missing."

"What about it?"

"You're tired," he said. "You've come a very long journey. You aren't thinking as fast as you might. Suppose we all sit down and talk this over quietly. Then you can decide whether or not you really want to call the police. Alison, perhaps Brenda would like some coffee. She looks all in."

"I don't want anything," Brenda said. "I just want to get this matter of Brigid settled as quickly as possible."

"Right," he said. "I just didn't want to take advantage of you when you're so tired. But if that's how you want it . . ."

Brenda suddenly sat down. "I *am* very tired. I hate air travel. And I hate trouble and arguments. Why can't we settle this without fuss? You know Alison will have to give Brigid up to Adrian and me."

"We were just trying to settle the thing without fuss when you arrived," Bill said. "If you hadn't come—I'm not sure— we might even have decided to lose the shoelace quietly. But you've rather forced my hand, because I daren't let you get your hands on Brigid. D'you want me to tell you how Nina and I found the shoelace?"

Brenda undid the knot of her headscarf and shook her hair free.

"If you want to," she said.

"It means telling you what happened that afternoon when Jocelyn died."

"What d'you mean, Bill?" Alison had just sat down at a table with her elbows on it and her head resting on one hand, her blazing hair cascading around her shoulders. "It was an accident, wasn't it?" She waited a moment for an answer, then said more loudly, "*Wasn't it an accident?*"

"It could have been," Bill said. "It just could have been. But then again, perhaps it wasn't. Listen, I'll tell you what happened. We all went down to the river to swim, all except mother and father, who went straight off to have a sleep. We all went into the river except Nicola, who sat and watched us for a little while, then went quietly back to the house. Jocelyn stayed with the rest of us till we all went back together. When he got to his room, Nicola was gone. Perhaps he knew she would be, perhaps not. We'll never know that for certain. What we do know is that when Nicola got back to the house, she got your car keys, Brenda, grabbed what she wanted from Jocelyn's wallet, packed her things, and left. And of course, whether or not he was expecting it, Jocelyn knew what had happened as soon as he got up to their room and found she wasn't there. So what did he do? It would have been very important for him to behave normally. I think the first thing he'd have done would have been to go to your room to ask you if your car keys were actually missing. And when you found they were, he'd have gone down to the garage to check on whether or not the car was missing too. And I think you went with him, to check on that yourself. And the car was gone, sure enough. So Jocelyn said he wanted to do some thinking and wandered off to the river. And because Ruth and Ern were on the verandah, he went by the path behind the bushes. And seeing him go off like that, you did some quick thinking and you followed him."

Brenda gave a long yawn. "I wish I had, Bill, I only wish I had. But none of this happened, you know. I didn't see him go. I was in my room, probably sound asleep already. And so was Adrian. I didn't know anything about Nicola having taken off until Nina and I went to look for her, after they'd found Jocelyn dead."

Bill shook his head. "You were down by the garage, and you were still in your bathers. But Ruth had hung up most of our things on those lines outside the kitchen door and Nina's red wrap was there and you grabbed it and put it on. If anyone saw you through the bushes, they'd see the red and think it was Nina. And of course, it might have been Nina but for one thing. When Jocelyn found Nicola was gone he wouldn't have gone to Nina to find out if the car keys were missing, he'd have gone to you. It would have been you who went down to the garage with him to check that the car was gone and who thought of following him down the path, thinking of that cliff and how easy it would be to push someone over there. It was you who'd a motive for wanting him dead. You'd forgotten that Brigid might still be alive. It was quite a shock to you when I reminded you that she might be. You liked the idea of inheriting his money and that lovely old house I've often heard you talk about. It must be worth an immense amount now."

Brenda brushed a hand wearily across her face as if she were brushing clinging cobwebs away.

"I don't understand a word of this. What about that shoelace?"

"Didn't you know you'd picked it up?" Bill said. "Did you do it automatically? Somewhere along the path it dropped out of Jocelyn's shoe and you saw it as you followed him and you picked it up and tucked it into the pocket of Nina's wrap. Whoever was wearing that wrap was the one who followed him, Brenda, and you're the only one who's small enough to have worn it."

Alison gave a choking little moan. "She killed him, did she, she really killed him?"

"Yes, she snatched her moment, just as he snatched his moments for his attacks on Nicola," Bill said. "There he was at the top of the cliff and she gave him a push and knocked him into the river. Of course she wouldn't have been strong enough to do it if he'd been on his guard, but he was taken by surprise and he just fell in. And naturally he hit his head hard on the rocks and was stunned. Then—what did you do then, Brenda? Did you go in yourself and swim along to him and hold him under until you were sure he was drowned, or did you leave it to chance? Somehow I don't see you leaving it to chance. Adrian knows, of course. He must, because he gave you an alibi which he must have known was false. And when he seemed to be clinging to you afterwards, he was really reassuring you that you could count on him. He's always done anything you wanted."

Brenda sprang up suddenly, shaking clenched fists at him, and shouting, "Leave Adrian out of this! It's lies, all lies! You haven't said a single thing you can prove. Jocelyn's death was an accident."

"No," Bill said.

"If it wasn't, Nicola killed him."

"No, that's what we were supposed to think if the question of murder ever arose. Nicola's flight was to be taken as a confession of guilt. I think it was that flight of hers that put it into your head that you'd found the right time to kill Jocelyn. But Nicola must have stolen the car keys from your handbag before you got back to your room from swimming, and once she'd got them, why should she stick around? She wouldn't have waited for Jocelyn to get back; she'd have gone as soon as she could get her things together. And she never picked up that shoelace or put on Nina's wrap. She was much too big to get into it."

Brenda gave a laugh, sinking back onto her chair.

"And that's all?" she said. "Try telling that to the police, Bill. Go home and try telling it to your Sergeant Furness. I don't think he'll be impressed. But the police here are going to listen to me when I tell them where to find Brigid and that you and Nina were entering into a conspiracy to protect your sister from the consequences of her wickedness. You aren't going to frighten me into silence with a lot of silly lies. No, Bill, oh no!" She laughed again. It was wild harsh laughter, mounting out of control.

Alison seemed suddenly unable to bear the sound of it. She pounded on the table before her with her fists.

"It isn't lies!" she cried. "It's true, you killed my love!"

179

"Try to convince anybody—*anybody!*" Brenda gasped through her laughter.

"*I* am convinced," Alison said.

And there was a gun in her hand.

It was a little weapon that had come out of the drawer of the table at which she was sitting. It was pointed at Brenda and the hand holding it was steady. Alison's face was without expression. It was also without beauty, an aged, cold, sick face that seemed to have no connection with the young body of the girl sitting there.

There was silence in the room for an instant till Brigid, feeling the terror in the room, gave a wail.

Bill lunged forward.

But before he could reach her, Alison had pulled the trigger. Brenda screamed, crumpled in her chair, then slowly toppled over sideways to the floor.

Laying the gun down on the table, Alison sat there quietly looking at what she had done. Then a very faint expression of satisfaction crept into her eyes.

"She's dead, isn't she?" she said. "I had to do it, of course, because she was quite right, Bill. No one would have believed you."

Chapter Fourteen

It was Alison herself, a few minutes later, who picked up the telephone and asked the police to come. No one else had tried to do it for her. For a little while she had gone on sitting motionless at the table, the gun lying disregarded on it, and had watched with uninterested eyes as Nina went down on her knees beside Brenda and Bill stooped over her then straightened up, making a gesture of hopelessness. Brigid had screamed with shock at the incomprehensible things that were happening around her. Then Alison had reached for the telephone, asked for the police, and when she had been connected with them, requested in a cool tone that someone should come as soon as possible to her address as someone had just been killed there.

In the middle of what she was saying, Bill made a movement as if he wanted to stop her before she committed herself too far, but then he turned away to the window, looking down into the mews. He seemed impatient now for the police to arrive.

Nina, still crouching beside Brenda, listened to the girl at the telephone with horror-struck fascination. The tone of Alison's voice might have been that of a telephone operator, it sounded so unconcerned with what she was saying. Her pose was relaxed, her expression was empty. It was shock, of course, and at any moment might dissolve into tears and screams. It would be less frightening, Nina thought, than this deadly calm. For what she was looking at now, she felt, was the face of a destroyer. The face of someone who destroyed without compunction, without premeditation, without thought. The destroyer not only of the woman who lay dead in front of her, but of Jocelyn and Nicola as well.

Or was that putting things the wrong way round? Was Alison herself the victim of Jocelyn and Nicola and their failure with one another? Was her only desire now to destroy herself? The gun lay very close to her hand. Would she use it again?

However, the police car turned into the mews and stopped at the pale blue door and the bell was rung and Bill went downstairs to answer it and Alison did not move in her chair. But as soon as the two policemen came into the room she began to talk. She talked on and on. Nothing could stop her. She talked with complete lucidity, as if this were a story that she had rehearsed many times in her mind, so that she knew exactly how to tell it and which she felt an immense pressure to tell.

She began with her first meeting with Jocelyn nearly two years ago in Elderwood, told how they had spent a week together in Sydney, had agreed to marry, then how he had written to her from England, telling her that he had married Nicola, and how she had made up her mind to follow him to England, certain that she could break the marriage up if she could see him again.

One of the policemen, who had taken charge of the gun, tried several times to check her, wanting to know who Brenda was and what had happened in this room. Bill also tried to stop Alison, telling her that she should say nothing at all until he had called a solicitor. But she talked inexorably on, merely impatient with their interruptions, telling how she and Jocelyn had concocted their plan to abduct Brigid and get rid of Nicola and marry after all. But Brenda had interfered. She had killed Jocelyn. She had ruined everything. She had deserved to die.

Nina had taken Brigid on her lap and was keeping her as quiet as possible. By shooting Brenda, Nina thought, Alison had probably saved Brigid's life. There was that quite important thing to be said for her.

The policeman, confused by Alison's very clarity, decided at that point to make a report to his superiors and spoke to the police station on his radio. He also warned Alison that she was not obliged to tell him anything, but that what she said could be taken down and used in evidence. She frowned until he stopped, then took up her story again.

Again he interrupted, "That's the Foley baby, then?"

"We think so," Nina said.

"She'll have to be formally identified, you know."

"I believe there are things here that belonged to her," she answered.

"But does she belong anywhere? Has she got any relatives left?"

"Her mother had a sister who more or less brought her up. She's married, with several children. She may take her on."

"Does she live in London?"

"Yes, in Richmond."

"We'll have to get in touch with her. Poor kid, no one seems to have done much caring about what was best for her, do they? Yet the whole thing seems to have been on her account. Can you give me her aunt's name and address?"

But before Nicola's sister was called, a young policewoman, who arrived with the detective superintendent and the sergeant who presently drove into the mews, took charge of

183

Brigid, and when the police surgeon and the photographer arrived too, she was taken away to the police station with Alison, Bill, and Nina.

Alison was still talking to anyone who would listen to her, having begun her story at the beginning again, repeating it almost word for word as she had told it before.

The superintendent interrupted her to ask how she had obtained a gun.

"From someone I know," she said. "I know all sorts of people. Useful people."

"Why did you want a gun?" he asked.

"I thought it would be best to have one, once Jocelyn brought Brigid to me," she said. "I thought I might have to protect myself against Nicola, if she ever found out about me. Or if anyone else had found out, they might have tried to blackmail me. I knew the whole situation was very dangerous. And sometimes I thought I might use it on myself. When I heard Jocelyn was dead, I nearly used it then. But someone had to look after Brigid. And now that I haven't got to worry about that, I do want everyone to understand how it all happened. I want them to understand what a wonderful love Jocelyn and I had. Now where was I? Oh yes, I was telling you about how I decided to come to England. . . ."

She was off again, the only sign that she was near to cracking up being a tendency to ramble in her story, to grow increasingly incoherent.

At the police station she was asked if she wanted to make a statement, and Bill again tried to interfere, demanding the presence of a solicitor. But Alison brushed this aside, saying that what she wanted more than anything else was to make a statement. She was taken away by a policewoman and went without even looking at Bill to say good-bye.

Some time later, first Bill, then Nina, were asked to make

statements and to sign them. It took a very long time. The police made a telephone call to Nicola's sister, Jennifer, who said that she would come at once, and this meant more waiting.

When Jennifer arrived she had her husband with her. Hugh Storey was a partner in a big firm of chartered accountants. He was a quiet, rather stolid-looking man, a little portly already at forty and slightly bald, but with very alert, kindly brown eyes behind his spectacles. Jennifer Storey was in some ways very like Nicola. She was dark and plump, with big, luminous dark eyes. But she was smaller, more compact, more reposeful. She controlled her own small world with calm and confidence. When she and Hugh had talked at length to the police, they came up to Nina and Bill, and Jennifer took Nina's hand.

"They won't let us take Brigid home with us," Jennifer said. "There are all sorts of formalities. But we'll have her as soon as we can and we'll do our best for her. I told the boys before we left that we might be bringing a new sister home with us and they just looked me up and down and said they didn't believe it." She smiled, but wanly, as if she did not feel sure that a smile of any kind was in order just then. "But you'll see, they'll love her, and so shall we. We've always wanted a daughter. So don't worry about her, Nina—and, Mr. Lyndon, don't worry because of what's happened. We'll see that Brigid survives it all. But I'm very sorry about your sister. What a trail of devastation that man Jocelyn left behind him. I never liked him much. I never trusted him, did I, Hugh?"

Hugh Storey gave an ambiguous little shake of the head, as if he thought that perhaps his wife had not always been as clear-sighted about her brother-in-law as she now believed.

"That's beside the point, isn't it?" he said. "The main thing is, Brigid's safe. We thought we'd never see her again."

"You must come and see her as soon as she's settled in with us," Jennifer said. "Both of you. Or are you going straight back to Australia, Mr. Lyndon?"

"I'm not sure," Bill said with a quick glance at Nina. "Sometime soon, I expect. But I'm not sure just when."

"Come and see us then," Jennifer said again.

He said that they would and the Storeys left.

"Nice people," Bill said when they had gone. "You know, I shouldn't be surprised if Brigid does better with those two than she would have with her own parents. And with ready-made brothers and all. Perhaps I'll get some sleep tonight after all. Let's go now. I think they're finished with us."

No one stopped them. It was late evening. The rush-hour crowds had gone and the streets were quiet. A little half-hearted snow . . .